Wishing on the Water

By Elizabeth York

General editing by Laura Hampton at Editing for You,
and Steve Czach

Editor in chief by Rosa Sophia

ISBN: 9780692420430

I was asked if I was capable of writing anything softer than Surviving Brooklyn. This is the softest I can get. Maybe one day I can give you a one-book-HEA, but since there are so many other books out there like that I would rather give you an adventure. This book is for those of you who asked for the softer side of me.

For my honor roll

AUSTIN- You are my oldest son & the apple of my eye. I don't know how you are or where you are, but I do know that my heart is with you wherever you are. There is not a day that goes by that I do not think of you. You are so much like your grandfather that I know that whatever is happening in your life that you will be alright because you wouldn't have it any other way. One day I hope when you look me up you will read this & know I have always and will always love you!

ALYSSA- You were always my rock star. You always knew what you wanted & never stopped till you got it. I see so much of me in you with the sacrifices you make for your family. You are growing up to be a wonderful lady with a beautiful soul. In the evilness of the world it is easy to lose your way, never change who you are because of that. Keep your kindness & your civility. I love you more than there are stars in the sky & never forget that they don't hold your wishes. The water holds our wishes.

ASHTON- My bouncing baby boy. Every single day I hug you & tell you I love you. Every single day I tell you that you are so very special to me, and I do that because you were born with a mature soul. You were just a little boy when life changed & it made you grow up entirely too fast so take this advice & run with it. Go to Chik-fil-A & slide down the slide, go to the nearest grocery store and throw a pop tart, go to the nearest lake and just stick your toe in, call a friend and have a water balloon fight, or even make a wish on the dandelion you blow on in the yard. Do whatever it takes to get some of that childishness back and enjoy because being a grown up can suck. I love you!

I love the three of you more than my own life. You are the air I breathe. I thought my life was full until I had you and then I realized I had been missing the greatest gift of all. The gift of three mini-me's. I love you all and hope one day you will read this and be as proud of me as I am of you.

Dear Daddy,

I stopped calling you "Jimmy" as that fateful day
came near.
I realized you were leaving me and there was nothing
more I feared.
You used to spoil me rotten with all your love and care.
But now each time I look for you.
My heart breaks for you are no longer here.
I knew that it was coming and that we
would have to say goodbye
But I wasn't ready when that day arrived.
Call me selfish daddy, but I still need you here.
To hold me, to love me, to always keep me near.
This light shines brightly for you daddy
in recognition for all that you had to do.
There will never be another daddy,
quite as loved as you.
I still need you here daddy, to help see me through
But since your gone all I can say is
It was an honor to have spend my days with you...
- Elizabeth York

Support Cancer Awareness

You are gone, but never forgotten

THE FINAL INSPECTION

The soldier stood and faced God, Which must always come to pass.
He hoped his shoes were shining, just as brightly as his brass.
"Step forward now, you soldier, how shall I deal with you?
Have you always turned the other cheek?
To My Church have you been true?"
The soldier squared his shoulders and said,
"No, Lord, I guess I ain't. Because those of us who carry guns,
Can't always be a saint. I've had to work most Sundays,
And at times my talk was tough. And sometimes I've been violent,
Because the world is awfully rough.
But, I never took a penny, that wasn't mine to keep...
Though I worked a lot of overtime, when the bills got just too steep.
And I never passed a cry for help, though at times I shook with fear.
And sometimes, God, forgive me, I've wept unmanly tears.
I know I don't deserve a place, among the people here.
They never wanted me around, except to calm their fears.
If you've a place for me here, Lord, It needn't be so grand.
I never expected or had too much, but if you don't, I'll understand."
There was a silence all around the throne,
Where the saints had often trod. As the soldier waited quietly,
For the judgment of his God.
"Step forward now, you soldier, you've borne your burdens well.
Walk peacefully on Heaven's streets, you've done your time in Hell."
~Author Unknown~

Chapter one

"Come on, Candice, we need to take our seats."

I was not aware of anything except that I was staring at my fiancé lying in a coffin. How could this be possible? I had just talked to him. We went to cake tastings last week. I reached down and fixed the sleeve of his policeman's jacket. I sensed a peacefulness to him, but there was none within me. I was devastated.

How many times had I wished him dead when we played together on the playground as kids? He made me eat dirt and pulled my hair and I wished for some divine intervention to make him go away.

I did not mean it. I take it back.

"Candice, we need to move and let the others see him before the service starts."

My best friend Christina was ushering me into a seat. I had no fight in me at the moment and I let her steer me away. The police chaplain urged everyone to take their seats as the services were about to begin. Beside me, my fiancé's mother wept uncontrollably.

I took her hand in mine and whispered,

"Michelle, I am here for anything you need." I tried to offer a smile as tears filled my eyes.

"I just miss him. He is happy with his dad in Heaven now, but I selfishly want them both here with me." Michelle's brittle voice broke as she cried into the tissue she held. I squeezed her free hand and rubbed her back.

I looked around the church and saw his fellow policemen wearing the same uniform he had on. They had taken up every pew in the church and still they lined the walls. They were casting looks of sorrow and sympathy toward me.

Trying to stay strong was disabling my ability to be supportive to others. I felt like someone had stolen my lifelines and left me in the ocean to drown. I watched as the men nodded to each other and I knew they were talking about me.

The chaplain began speaking to the crowd as people continued to file into the church. I placed my hands on my lap and bowed my head as he began the prayer. I didn't hear another word that was spoken. I was numb to the core. This wasn't real. His partner, Jaxson, wasn't even here yet. They would never bury Chase without his partner here to say goodbye.

Movement caught my attention, and I watched as the men came forward and closed the casket. Elvis's version of "Go Rest High On That

Mountain" played in the background.

I hadn't even noticed that Christina had left my side until I looked for her. I saw her over in the corner lighting a white candle for Chase, tears pouring from her eyes. I didn't remember her even liking Chase, but she was there.

When the commissioner came and held his hand out for us, I stood and walked with Michelle to the closed casket. I put my hand on top. This was supposed to be goodbye, yet I felt as though he was still with me. The thought of him gone left me breathless, and my chest tightened. I was in a panic as I couldn't bring my heart to say goodbye. I felt a hand on the small of my back and turned my head as I gasped and stared into the stormy gray eyes I had known for most of my life. It was Chase's partner and best friend, Jax.

"Candice, are you okay?" He took hold of me and rubbed my back. I felt like I was being suffocated in the church. I had hidden my tears and feelings for days, but with Jax finally here I was going to crumble.

"Jax, I can't..." I couldn't even finish what I was trying to say. He was my lifeline and was always in tune with what I needed. I was grateful that he was my best friend.

Jax was in his policeman's dress uniform. The same uniform I was burying my fiancé in. The thought flashed through my mind that I was lucky I hadn't lost both of them, followed by the fear of what would happen if Jax died, too. Suddenly I felt weak. I swayed as Jax pulled me closer and walked me out of the church. I heard people murmuring, "Poor girl," and "She will never move on." I didn't want the snickers or sympathy. I just wanted to breathe through the suffocation of my broken heart.

"It's all right, Candy. You don't have to be the strong one holding everyone together right now," Jax said as he walked me out of the church.

We stood outside under an old oak tree. I wrapped my arms around him with my face leaning on his chest, facing the front door of the church. I didn't try to move. Jax held me tightly against him. I drenched his jacket in tears, but I don't think he cared.

"I can't do this," I mumbled. "I can't let him go."

"Candy, you and I will get through this together. I won't leave your side until you tell me to."

I forcefully slowed my breathing and calmed my tears. I still had an entire day ahead of me, a day of admitting the love of my life was gone. I knew I wasn't the only one who'd lost Chase, but I could only deal with one heartache at a time.

"Where were you?" I asked as I pulled myself together.

"Last minute lead. I wanted to see where it went."

"Did you catch him?" I whispered, not knowing if I really wanted the answer. Did I really want to know who shot my fiancé? Did I really want to watch him stand trial? Chase had been gunned down, and I would have to hope the bastard who did it would spend his life in prison.

"No. It was a bad lead, but I will find him," Jax whispered as he laid a soft kiss on top of my head.

"How are you doing, Jax. Really?" I asked, hoping he was doing better than I was. He seemed to be holding himself together, but I could tell he was crushed.

"I will be all right. I'm more worried about you. We have each other and we will get through this together," he assured me.

Voices near the door grew louder.

Jax remained stoic as people filed out. He'd put his emotions aside to be there for me, and for that I would be eternally grateful. I watched the door of the church as everyone emerged and shared tearful embraces. I was supposed to be there next to Michelle, but I couldn't handle it. I needed comfort from Jax. All I wanted at the moment was my best friend.

"Candice, do you want me to take you home?" Jax asked.

"N-no. I have to go. It's my duty to Chase and his family." I watched tears stream down the cheeks of all the people who loved Chase.

"Candice, you don't have to do anything you don't want to. Do *not* add any extra heartache for yourself."

"Just hold my hand, Jax."

As the church finished letting everyone out, the officers carried out the casket and placed it in the buggy that was led by a white horse. This was the one thing Chase had asked for in his will.

One last ride as a knight in shining armor.

I watched as the men saluted the casket as the horse pulled the carriage forward. Then the family followed behind it and we walked in silence as the bagpipes played.

"Jax, do you think you could stay with me tonight?" I asked in a whisper. I didn't want to seem vulnerable, but I was. Going back to the house alone, the house Chase and I had just bought together, seemed like a punishment.

"Why don't you come stay in my guest room? We can order take out and watch movies if you like. We can do whatever you want."

I nodded my acceptance. I don't know why I was feeling afraid to ask Jax for anything. Perhaps the grieving was interfering with my actions.

Jax was the calm to my storm. Every fight Chase and I had, I went to Jaxson and would spill my guts as to whether I thought I was right or wrong. Chase would call him and tell him his version, while I was driving over there. He acted as our own personal marriage counselor.

The bagpipes wailed "Amazing Grace" as we marched the few blocks to the cemetery. The sound alone sent shivers down my spine. I was surrounded by hundreds of people, but I felt alone.

I was grateful Christina was here even though she didn't like Chase that much. She had really stepped up when it came to helping me put everything together. I turned to find her and saw her long red hair first. She stood beside Chase's mom, Michelle. Her green eyes were red-rimmed and she seemed to be sick. She clutched her stomach with one hand while holding Michelle's hand with the other.

"You all right?" I asked Christina in a hushed whisper.

"Funerals always upset me. I will be fine. How

are you holding up?"

"I'll be okay," I whispered, and Christina nodded.

We approached the hill and slowly climbed it as we walked to Chase's final resting place. I had gotten him a plot that overlooked the river up on the hill and a red oak tree shaded his spot. I thought it was perfect for him.

His large, black etched tombstone read: *Chase Henry Matson, beloved son, brother, friend, partner, and fiancé.* It really fit what Chase wanted. I had done everything he asked, except for burying him with his guns. The department had a policy against it. Since I couldn't do that, I had a nine millimeter engraved into each corner of the tombstone instead.

My brain faded into memories as we filed into a tent with chairs. We took our seats as the commissioner stepped up to say a few words about honor, dedication, and sacrifice. I don't know why I didn't like him, but he rubbed me the wrong way.

I leaned on Jax's arm as the chaplain stepped up to talk about religion and how Chase was walking the path in Heaven. I tried to listen, but the words faded out. I was in a world of my own and no one else was there.

I jumped at the first rifle shot. It brought me back to reality and made me startle again for the second and third as they finished the three-volley salute.

The sound of "Taps" came from the bagpipes immediately afterward. Chills wracked my body as the realization came that this was it; I would never see Chase again. A stray tear fell as I listened and waited. Jax held my hand and gave it a squeeze, reminding me he was still with me. I was grateful to have him there to lean on.

They lowered the casket, and Michelle was the first one to take the shovel and pour dirt on him, followed by the rest of the family. I waited until they were done, then I picked up a rose they had set aside and stood before the hole in the ground.

"Chase, I have loved you for years. I do not know how to move on or breathe anymore because you were my air and my reason for getting up every morning. I will love you all day, every day for the rest of my life."

I tossed the rose into the hole and whispered, "Goodbye, Chase." Jax stepped up and we took turns with the shovel, dropping the dirt into the hole and watching it land on the casket.

The chaplain prayed as I sat back down, and the funeral came to an end. It was time for the toasting farewell. I had never heard of a toasting farewell until my mom's funeral. People went to dinner and everyone ordered a shot, then drank to her arrival in Heaven. They drank to her no longer being in pain. They drank to seeing her again one day. I wondered what the point was, but it seemed to help my dad, so I went along with it and toasted "cheers" with the cup of apple juice I held.

"You ready to go to the farewell?" Jax asked.

"Ready as I will ever be."

"You don't have to go, Candice. It's not mandatory," Jax whispered, but it really *was* mandatory. How could I ignore his family and fellow officers due to my own pain?

"I am ready, but do me a favor. Don't leave my side. I don't want to be left alone right now."

Jax nodded, and we headed back to the church parking lot, where the limo was waiting to take us downtown to the banquet hall where the toasting farewell would be held.

Chapter Two

As we walked inside the banquet hall, I went to the bar immediately with Jax. The room was too bright for a toasting farewell. The white walls and beige tiled floors gave it a light ambiance, and my mood was the opposite.

We both ordered an Irish whiskey, and I swirled my drink in the glass. I wondered what I was going to say. What am I supposed to say? I thought back to the lovely words my dad had said about my mom. He had talked about love and marriage. He talked about my mom's plans and how I was her greatest gift.

I was getting emotional thinking about my mom when I was supposed to be grieving for Chase. I was officially screwed up.

I looked to Jax, who was shaking hands with a man in a black suit. I didn't know who he was, but he looked important. I tried to give them privacy and walk away, but Jax tightened his grip on my hand.

Michelle came up and I put my glass down as I gave her a one-armed hug. She was waiting for me to say my toast to Chase so that she could go home and rest. Having your heart broken and being around a lot of grief is exhausting.

I looked back to find Jax staring at me. I nodded to him that it was time, and headed toward the framed picture of Chase at the front of the room. As I stood there a moment and contemplated what I was going to say, I heard the whispers that fell around me. Jax squeezed my hand, an added reminder that I wasn't alone even if it felt that way.

"I would like to thank all of you for coming today to pay respects to Chase," I began. *"Somewhere in the back of my head, I waited for him to sit up and tell me it was another one of his stupid practical jokes. We know how much he loved those, and I probably would've broken his nose for this one. I...It wasn't until we closed the casket that I realized he wasn't getting up. This isn't some awful joke.*

"I have loved the guy for my whole life. I am turning twenty-five this year and just told Chase twenty-four years was a long time to wait for him to propose. He laughed and said we had our whole lives to be together. I don't think Chase knew his time would be cut so short, but even if he did, he lived each day to the fullest. Always out saving the world one criminal at a time. He was never one to be idle and I loved that about him.

"I came here today to say goodbye to my very best

friend and the love of my life, but I can't...so I lift my glass to celebrate the life of the most wonderful man I have ever known and hope that he waits for me to join him in Heaven. This may be a farewell toast, but I am only drinking a see-you-later shot."

We took our shot as others applauded or drank their drink and then we walked to the bar for the next one as Chase's uncle stepped up with Michelle. Movement caught my eye and I saw my dad. He gave a nod as if to say hello and tried to give me a half smile, but I knew he was hurting. Chase had been like a son to him.

I tugged on Jax's hand, removing him from the conversation with Chase's uncle and pulled him out the back door. We stepped out on the large octagon shaped deck. I just needed fresh air, and wanted to get away from all the broken hearts. I secretly wished I could say something and make it better. I would give anything to see Michelle with dry eyes and a smile on her face.

"Let me take you home," Jax offered, but I shook my head. We walked out to the edge of the deck that extended over the river. I leaned on the railing to look into the water.

"Jax," I said, sniffling. "Do you remember when the city tore down our wishing well?"

"I remember, Candice. I remember you were determined to have a place to make a wish and the stars just wouldn't do."

I leaned my head against him and reminisced for a moment about three little kids who set out on an adventure to find a new place to wish. We couldn't have been more than seven years old. It was about the time my mom got sick.

"I was always told never to wish on the first star at night. If everyone wishes on one star, how will the star keep up? A star with too many wishes will just fall out of the sky. Raindrops are plentiful, and there are thousands. They wash away the filth and carry it to a better place. So when you make a wish, wish on the water and let it carry your problems away."

Jax wrapped his arms around me as my back rested on his chest and my head fell against his shoulder. He was warm and comforting. He'd put up a shield around his own emotions and stepped up to take care of me.

"Who told you about wishing on the water?" Jax whispered in my ear.

"My mom."

There was a silent pause. My mom had died of cancer when I was little. Even now, after all these years, it was still a sore spot. I missed her and still mourned for her to the point that if someone brought her up, chances were I would shed a tear.

Grieving came in waves. Sometimes I would be perfectly fine. Other days I would drown in the need to see her or hold her. When it got really bad, I would go to my mom's grave and talk to her. I would spend hours in the grass next to her. Now I would have to visit Chase there as well.

"I remember when we found this lake, Candice. You were a tiny little thing. So beautiful with your brown hair in a ponytail. Your bright blue eyes would stare right through me as if you knew all my secrets. I remember fighting with Chase over you, but I let him have you because it was what you wanted and he was always a better man than me."

I didn't know any of that, but it was nice to remember the good times we'd had with Chase. I thought it was sweet to hear the boys fight over me at such a young age. I remember thinking the three of us would be together forever. I turned and put my head against Jax's heart, wrapping my arms around him.

"It's my fault. I was supposed to go first that day. I got a flat on the way to court and Chase told me he would go first so I had some time. I wasn't there."

I watched as he tried his best to keep his emotions at bay. I tightened my grip and stared into his stormy eyes, now slightly swollen and red. He was holding back more than I thought. I never once thought he would blame himself. They knew Chase had been targeted. He had received so many threats after taking on an undercover assignment that had been blown.

"Jax, you know it wasn't you. Chase got threats he didn't tell anyone about. You didn't do this. It is not your fault."

"I was there for his last words, but I wasn't there to save him. I should have been there. I would have laid down my life for him. I wish..." He broke the sentence with the words stuck inside him and stared at the water. I closed my eyes and hoped he was wishing on the water for himself, and not to trade his life for Chase's.

I took his hand and walked along the river's edge.

"You're my best friend, Jax," I whispered as we walked toward the sunset.

"And you are mine, Candy." He spoke with a softened tone. I could hear the emotions being held back in the slight break in his voice.

"I love you, Jax." I pulled him into a hug and wrapped my arms around his neck, laying my head on his chest, listening to his heartbeat. It was soothing to hear his heart pumping blood. It is amazing the things you come to realize you will miss when someone dies. I would miss Chase's heartbeat when we snuggled on the couch.

"Candice, everything will be all right. I will catch the bastard who did this, and Chase's memory will always live on inside us. Just don't ever abandon our friendship."

"Why would you say that?" I asked, because the last thing he'd said had me confused.

"Candy, when your mom died, you and your dad abandoned each other. You lived in the same house, but you were practically strangers. Chase and I were closer to your dad than you were. I just want to make sure that doesn't happen to us."

"It won't, Jax. I promise."

There was nothing left to say. Our emotions were cut open and left to bleed out as we sought comfort in each other. I relished the warmth from his touch and I wanted to believe I gave him the same, but he was the strong, silent type and I would never know if I was helping or hindering.

He took my hand and we walked for a while. Occasionally we would stop and stand side by side by the water, making wishes on the water. We followed the trail for what seemed like hours until we reached the lighthouse that stood off the rocks next to where the inlet emptied into the ocean. Whenever I wept, Jax and I were able to lean on each other without a word being said. I was grateful we could just be with each other like this.

We watched as the sun set over the lighthouse, the waves crashed on the shore, and the winds howled from a storm somewhere off in the distance. Right there, I made a wish on the water—that both Jax and I would find happiness one day. We deserved to smile again.

Chapter Three

Two weeks had passed and I still felt as though I couldn't breathe. I refused to go home to the cold, empty house I once shared with Chase. Jax had been kind enough to let me sleep in his room every night, holding me while I cried. I really was blessed to have him in my life.

I sat at Jax's desk and stared at the blank Microsoft Word page. Once upon a time, I won awards for my best-selling novels, but now I couldn't think of anything to say.

"Candice, why don't you take a break and come back to it later?" Jax called out from the kitchen where he was making us Tim Hortons' coffee for the afternoon.

"I need to write. I need to be able to move forward and get back to being myself."

Jax brought a mug of coffee over to the desk that sat in front of the window just to the right of the front door. The rain had stopped, but drops kept dripping off the gutter. This captivated my attention as Jax placed my coffee next to my laptop.

"You need to let it happen. If you force it, it won't flow," Jax stated as he leaned over and placed a kiss on the top of my head.

"What the hell do you know about being a writer?" I snapped. I was instantly angry and didn't understand why. I needed to hate him for no reason other than he was there.

"Come on, Candice. We're taking a ride."

Just when I was about to protest, I found myself being carried out to the truck. Jax put me in the seat of his white F-250. I crossed my arms, glaring as he buckled me in and shut the door.

He went back in the house and returned just as I was getting ready to get out of the truck. He had my laptop and a comforter in his hands. He locked the door to the house and then came out and placed everything in the back seat of his extended cab.

"Time to breathe, Candice," Jax said as he started the truck. I rolled my eyes and watched as he backed out of the driveway.

Jax had taken me to the cemetery every day to sit at the gravesite next to where they buried Chase. He even stayed while I talked to my mom's tombstone.

I assumed we were headed back to the cemetery so I turned and stared out the window of the truck as it sped out of the neighborhood. The constant vibration was making my eyelids heavy, and soon I drifted off to sleep.

"Wake up, Candice," I heard Jax say, but I didn't want to open my eyes. "Come on, stubborn ass." He chuckled, and my lips turned up with a smile. The smile hurt my face because it went against how I felt.

"*You* are the stubborn ass," I said with a hint of laughter as I opened my eyes to be met with Jax's gray eyes.

"Whatever. I am the rubber and you are the glue." He helped me out of the truck.

"Are we five years old again?" I asked as I caught a glimpse of childishness in his face.

"Yes, Candice, we are five years old, and there is nothing in the world that is holding us back, making us sad, or stopping us from living our lives."

I looked behind the truck at the park that sat across from the lighthouse where the inlet met the ocean. This was where I had first met Chase and Jax. The two ornery boys had caught my attention the minute my mother had let me out to play.

I saw the yellow weathered slide where Jax used to catch me as I slid down, and the ladder Chase helped me climb to slide down again. The multicolored merry-go-round was rusted and looked out of service.

The memories hit me like whiplash, and I wanted to be that little kid again. I wanted to have my pig-tails pulled and push the boys into the sand. I wanted to cry to my mother about them. She always said, "They'll hate you today, but love you tomorrow."

"Jax, it's all taped off," I whispered as the memories fled and I took in the dirty and torn down condition of the park.

"Not enough funding. They're going to tear it down rather than fix it. I heard they may put a restaurant here."

I walked toward the yellow caution tape. I could see the three little kids we used to be running laps around the bridge that carried us from one side of the playground to the other where the swings rested.

I went under the tape and headed across the sand to the swings. There was minimal rust on the swing set where, as teenagers, we had scratched our names in the metal pole.

I pulled my black flip-flops off and curled my toes in the sand that was still packed down from the rain. I used my arm to wipe the remaining water off the swing and sat down.

I relished the feel of being back in the swing as if I was a child that had the whole world ahead of her.

"Candy, want a push?" Jax asked, and I nodded. He began pushing me on the swing. I wished on the water that was on the chain. I wished I could just let it all go and not feel like I was drowning anymore. I wanted to be able to bask in the sunlight that was piercing through the gray clouds.

"Hey, Jax," I called out as he pushed me higher.

"What is it, baby girl?"

"In case there is no tomorrow, I want you to know I love you."

Jax caught the swing and brought it to a slow halt. He walked around in front of me and crouched down so we were at eye level. He placed one hand on my knee and gave me a comforting squeeze.

"Candy Cane, where did that come from?" He spoke softly and looked concerned.

"I just wanted you to know that I love you. You are my best friend, Jax. I don't know how I would ever cope without you in my life."

"I'm not going anywhere, Candice. I won't leave your side unless you don't want me in your life." Jax wiped away the tear that slid down my cheek.

"I have been thinking about it a lot and I need you to always be all right. I can't lose you too. I get scared that I am putting too much on you and that I may drown you in my grief or that you may get shot trying to find out who killed Chase."

"Candy, sweetheart, ease your mind. You are the only reason I get up in the morning. Spending the last two weeks with you has kept me going. You are my family, and nothing is going to change that. I told you I am never leaving your side unless you don't want or need me in your life."

"I think I told you I didn't want you in my life when we were about nine, but you're still here," I stated with a sniffle and a hint of laughter.

"That didn't count. I am sure you said it because I was being a dick." Jax chuckled as he rose to his feet. I stood up and reached into my pocket, pulling out a silver necklace I had been carrying around for weeks. I placed it in his hand.

"What is this, Candy?"

"It's Saint Michael," I explained. "I was doing research for a story when I read about how Saint Michael is the patron saint of police officers. He is supposed to protect you and keep you safe. There is even a policeman's prayer on the back."

Jax looked at the necklace and read the poem before looking back at me with concern evident on his face.

"Candice, what happened to Chase is not going to happen to me. You shouldn't worry so much."

I took the necklace back and unhooked the clasp, then reached up and fastened it around his neck so the saint was facing forward on his chest.

"I bought this right after Chase died. I knew if it could happen to him, it could happen to anyone. I know you may not want to wear this, but I need you to keep it on for me. Promise me you will never take it off."

"I promise, Candy Cane," Jax murmured before pulling me into his arms. He was so tall that he could rest his chin on the top of my head and that was exactly what he did.

"Jax, do you think we will ever feel normal again?"

He merely squeezed me tighter and I closed my eyes to soak up his warmth. I listened to his heart beat in his chest as he let out a deep breath.

"Candy, we are like this park. We have endured a beating, and we are now rusted and broken. We can either fix ourselves or let life demolish us. I think that as long as we have each other, time will help repair us."

"Jax, what would it take to save our park?" I asked, but the answer wouldn't come as Jax's phone rang. He let me go and I went back to swinging as Jax walked off with his phone glued to his ear. He stepped over to the big tree our names were carved into.

I really missed being a kid. I didn't have responsibilities, nor did I care about things that get under my skin now like taxes, deadlines, or death. I could be carefree.

Jax kept his back to me while he was on the phone which made me think that maybe there was a woman in his life I was holding him back from. I had been taking up all his time since Chase died, but I couldn't bear to be left alone. It might be about the case, though, and I wasn't privy to it.

I dug my feet into the wet sand and wiggled my toes just like I did as a kid. The winds picked up as the disturbance moved in behind the storm that had just left.

"Candice." Jax called my name and I pulled my feet out of the sand and stood up off the swing. He wore an expression that was hard to describe. It seemed like a mixture of pain and anger, tinged with guilt.

"What is it?" I asked as apprehension overwhelmed my body.

"That was Christina. We need to go to your house," Jax stated quietly and moved toward me. He looked at me as though I was going to shatter at any second.

"Jax, you're scaring me." He really hadn't said anything scary, but his tone said something was wrong.

"Candy Cane, I am not trying to scare you. I just don't know if you are ready for this."

"Ready for what?" The worst thoughts were running through my mind.

"Someone broke into your house and—"

I cut Jax off and turned to head for his truck. Someone had invaded my home, my privacy, and what was left of my life with Chase. I wasn't going to cry. The overwhelming anger coursing through my veins wouldn't let me.

How dare someone do that?

I think it was safe to say I had moved into the anger stage in the five stages of grief; the thought of someone in my house had me ready to punch something.

I climbed into the truck and slammed the door to look out the window and see Jax holding my flip-flops. I was losing it, too angry to care.

Chapter Four

Upon arrival at my house the anger had dwindled into shock as I saw people in uniform moving in and out in seemingly synchronized movements. Men wore gloves and carried bags while others dusted my door, which looked like it had been broken off its frame. They appeared as though they had done this a million times and it was nothing new.

Jax got out of the truck and walked around and opened the door for me. As soon as I stepped out of the truck, I felt out of place. I didn't belong here.

Christina was standing to one side of my gray brick house talking to a man in a suit. I had seen him at Chase's funeral, but all the faces and names had since blurred together. Christina took notes as the man talked. I had never seen her at work before. She was like an entirely different person, so serious and determined.

Jax took my hand as I stood outside his truck. Watching as people walked back and forth, the flashing lights from the police cars, all made this seem something out of the movies, or a twist I might put in a book. This stuff didn't happen in real life.

Jax gave my hand a squeeze and I walked with him over toward Christina. As soon as she saw me, the seriousness fell away. I watched as an almost forced sympathetic expression crossed her face as she headed right for me. She enveloped me in her arms and held me tight.

"Are you all right? Where have you been?" Christina asked, and I merely nodded my head in Jax's direction. Then she looked at his hand which was still holding mine. "Jax, so nice of you to drive her over, but I have it from here," Christina mumbled.

"Candy stays with me," Jax declared. There must have been some kind of pissing contest between the two of them that I was not aware of because they glared bitterly at each other.

"What happened?" I asked, trying to pull their focus away from each other and get this over with. I didn't want to stand here any longer than I had to, and their obvious distaste kept me rooted to this spot, watching.

"Someone broke in the front and back door," Christina answered.

"That seems a bit excessive to break both doors, doesn't it?" I asked, my voice barely above a whisper. The whole thing didn't compute. "What is missing?"

"We will have you do an inventory of anything that is missing after we are done processing the scene," Christina said a little too loudly, and then leaned in and whispered to both of us. "It doesn't look like anything is missing, but the house is trashed. It's *fubar.*"

"I don't want to be here," I muttered without even thinking. Now that I had their attention, though, maybe I could leave.

"Do you want to go in and see the damage? One of us can take you in there."

"Do I have to go in? Level with me, do I want to go inside?" I asked. Christina and Jax shared a look. They were having that silent we-wear-the-same-badge talk. It was annoying when Chase and Jax did it, but it was worse now.

"Candy, you don't want to go in there. Your house has been trashed. Everything was pulled out or tossed, from your kitchen items to your televisions and photo albums. Nothing was left untouched."

I dropped Jax's hand and walked toward the door. I didn't want to go inside, but some part of me felt like I needed to. I walked up the three steps to the porch and saw the fractured doorframe.

Inside, glass had been shattered everywhere. The television had been busted. Even the gas logs in the fireplace had holes in them. My photos from the albums on the shelf were torn into pieces and lying on the floor. I thought I was going to be sick.

I looked to the right and noticed one small shadow box still hanging on the wall right beside the front window. It was a frame I had bought. Inside, it held the first rose petal to fall from the first set of roses Chase ever bought me, and a four-leaf clover Jax had given me after we ventured into the woods to find a new place to wish. Both had been freeze-dried and mounted inside the little box.

This was all I had left of my relationship with

Chase. He was gone and so were his clothes, his pictures, and even his smell. Almost as though he never existed. I couldn't breathe as I hugged the shadow box to my chest.

"Candice, I am going to need you to step outside and talk to me while they finish clearing the scene."

That was all I needed to hear to walk out. It didn't have that comforting feeling most houses have. Now that Chase had died, it felt like a stranger's house. I wanted to sell it and start over in an apartment or brownstone closer to downtown, but the chaplain had given me his *Don't do anything for one-year* speech.

"Candy, you okay?" Jax asked as he reached for my arm to lead me out of the house.

"I am fine. I want to go back to your house if that is okay."

"Candice, are you going to be at Jax's later?" Christina asked in a monotone whisper. Her eyes looked inquisitive as if she was questioning something but her lip quivered just enough to notice.

"I will be there, why?"

"I wanted to see if I could come by. I haven't seen you in two weeks and I really want to talk to you. I want to know that you are doing all right. You seem to have cut everyone off except Jax, and while I am grateful you have him I still want you to be able to talk to me if you need it." She looked at Jax as if having that silent conversation again.

"Yeah, I will be there. You can come by anytime if it is all right with Jax. I do miss our girl talk."

Jax merely nodded, and I hugged Christina as we said our goodbyes. Everything in the house was a total loss. I didn't even bother looking back as we pulled away. I had the only thing left untouched and I would cherish this shadow box in whatever new apartment I got.

"How are you doing, sweetheart?" Jax asked as we pulled out of the neighborhood.

"It was worse than I expected," I said. I had expected everything they described, but seeing it was like a sucker punch to the gut. It had stolen my breath to find all our things like that.

"Christina is stepping out of undercover work to handle the breaking and entering. She will find out who and why. We will help you with the insurance claim and get it all cleaned up."

"Why is she doing that? I thought she only worked undercover or something." I really didn't know much about their work except what Chase would tell me and that was very little.

"She is sucking up to the commissioner and chief of police to transfer over to narcotics and try to become my new partner."

Jax's hands tightened on the wheel when he uttered the word *partner*. He was not ready for a new partner, and I didn't think the two of them would make a good team. They would constantly be fighting.

"What do you want, Jax?"

"I don't want a new partner." He gritted his teeth with the answer.

Seeing the house like that and hearing Jax's pain in his words brought reality back to me. I was feeling the loss of Chase like it was the first moment all over again. I had believed I was doing well, but then a wave of grief came out of nowhere and stole what semblance of sanity I had left.

Doing my best to hide my heartbreak as well as my tears, I was a survivor and needed to stay strong. At least, that is what I told myself every morning when I woke up to realize Chase wasn't coming home.

Chapter Five

We arrived at Jax's as the sun began setting and the day's heat had started to chill. He got a message and had to run to the precinct. Jax would need to eat, and I knew I could eat something, but the left over home-cooking comfort foods were out of the question. We had been surviving off them since the funeral and frankly I wanted something different. I thought it would be a nice surprise to have dinner waiting for him when he came back.

I called for Chinese food before I took a shower, then enjoyed the heat on my raw face. My eyes burned from how much I had rubbed them. My emotional hold broke the minute Jax left me alone to shower. I couldn't pretend I wasn't heartbroken; I just thought there were better ways of dealing with my broken heart than crying all the time. I turned off the shower in time to hear the doorbell. I grabbed a navy blue towel and wrapped it around me, hurrying for my purse.

I opened the door, greeted by Christina. I hadn't been expecting her. I ordered Chinese, not an emotional friend, and I was sure to start crying again. I'd become a wreck and just needed some space.

"Can we talk?" Christina whispered without meeting my eyes.

Phrases that began that way never ended well. I always cringed at those words. *Can we talk? Yeah, I hit your car. Can we talk? I killed your dog. Or, my favorite one. Can we talk? I hate you.* Whatever was at the end of her sentence wouldn't be good.

"You're early, but sure. Come in. Let me grab some clothes."

I had her sit on the gray couch in the living room. I ran up the stairs and grabbed Jax's *Theory of a Deadman* t-shirt. I donned it quickly and grabbed my black boy shorts and slid them on. I rubbed the towel through my hair, which made the brown curls I tried hard to hide come to life.

I ran down the stairs and stopped mid-step as she was on the phone crying. I stood frozen and listened to her part of the conversation.

"I am getting ready to tell her." Then there was a pause in the conversation. Christina got up to get a paper towel and wipe her eyes. Then she spoke again. "I think Candice can handle it." I stepped down and the step creaked. She saw me, saying her farewells on the phone, then returned to her seat on the couch.

I don't know who had upset her, but I was going to try to be the friend she would need me to be, even though I was a shattered mess.

I sat in the gray recliner that matched the couch and love-seat. I grabbed the remote and flicked on the fireplace that was across from the couch, since the late spring air was still getting chilly at night.

"So, Chris. What's going on?" I watched her rub her hands on her thighs. She seemed nervous, but she and I had been friends for nearly twenty years.

"I wasn't going to tell you. Bu-but...I just have to tell you now. Because I love you."

She was stuttering and refused to make eye contact. What could she have done? I waited as she got her words together. I was going to have to work on my impatience, because I wanted to shake her and ask her what it was.

"Candice, please know I love you and would never do anything purposely to hurt you."

I watched as tears streamed down her face. I didn't know what to do. Part of me wanted to comfort her while the other part warned me to wait. I had lost and buried my fiancé. I was sure whatever she had done wouldn't faze me.

"Chris, we have been friends forever. You can tell me anything. Just spit it out."

Jax walked in. He nodded in greeting as he carried his things upstairs. I waited and watched as she tried to find the words. When I heard footsteps again, I looked over to see Jax watching me with confusion in his eyes. The disdain he felt for Christina was evident as well. He looked as though he was studying her body language.

"Candice, I royally screwed up and I hurt you. I am so sorry. I would take it back if I could."

I couldn't figure out what she'd done to me. I still wanted to hear that part. Her eyes met mine and the look on her face spoke volumes of guilt, remorse, even sorrow. *What could she have done?* I glanced at Jax, who seemed more lost than I was.

"Chris, I don't know what you think you did. If you tell me, I could forgive you. I love you, Christina."

I watched as my words coursed over her. Each one seemed like a dagger to her heart.

What the hell?

Jax sat on the arm of the recliner waiting to hear about this mystery that had her in tears.

"Candice, I'm pregnant." She turned her face away from me. Not mad or angry, I was a little shocked, but genuinely happy for her.

"Why would you think I would be mad?"

She rubbed her hands on her pants again. Jax's impatience was clear as we waited. He placed a hand on my shoulder while Christina took an ultrasound out of her purse and passed it to me.

How cute. I wondered if it was a boy or girl. The date said she was about sixteen weeks.

Well, that was when they were undercover.

I wondered if Jax was the father. He must have known what I was thinking, because he shook his head no.

I started to hand it back, waiting for some kind of explanation as she wept hysterically. I would wait until she could talk to me. Maybe something was wrong with the baby. *Oh, I sure hope not.* I only wanted the best for Christina.

The doorbell rang. I got up and grabbed my wallet off the bar that separated the kitchen and living room. I went to the front door and paid for the Chinese food, then placed it on the black marble bar top that acted as a median. I turned back around to find Jax consoling her.

What the hell did I miss?

He wore an anxious look on his face when I returned to my seat. I was unsettled by that. No matter what happened I was always okay with Chase and Jax. The look on his face caused me to shiver, even with the heat of the fire. Christina still averted her gaze, and Jax picked up the ultrasound off the coffee table.

"Candice." He froze on his words. Why couldn't anyone talk around me? Was it because they thought I would break again? I was holding my own and damn proud I wasn't crumbling again. I could handle it.

"Guys, come on now, it's worse the longer you wait." I felt like I was being left out of a secret.

I watched in slow motion as Jax nodded to Christina, setting the ultrasound back down. He then got up with his giant six-foot body and came to stand in front of me. I peered up at him and he lifted me out of his chair. I waited as he sat back down in the chair, placing me in his lap with his hands around my waist.

I had seen him do this before. Forcing me into his lap when he thought I was ready to fight some girl in a bar for messing with them. Chase did the same thing. I gave kisses; they held people down. I made a mental note to address the aggressive way in which he adds to the bad news later.

"Candice, I...we named the baby." There was a hesitation in her voice, as if she might be reconsidering. I reached for it on the coffee table and looked for the name.

BABY GIRL MATSON, CHELLE

Sitting in Jax's lap did nothing for my comfort. My skin grew cold as I stared at the last name of the baby. The baby's had Chase's last name. *What the fuck?*

I looked at her, and the realization hit me. I wanted to attack her and tried, but a big burly man was holding me in his lap while I fought to get free.

"What the fuck, Christina?" I screamed at her. I wiggled and fought as I tried to get loose, but Jax was too strong. "Let me go, Jax!" I screamed as I clawed and smacked him. "You we're supposed to be my friend. Friends don't do this to each other!" I yelled as my anger raged through me.

"Candice, please!" Christina shouted over me.

"Fuck you!" I lunged for her again, but Jax wouldn't let me go.

I kicked and screamed until I was tired and the fight was replaced with anguish. I watched as Jax's muscles relaxed a moment as I fell back on him and the tears started to fall.

"Candice, it is not what you think. We had to." She looked straight at me with that comment and I wanted to spit on her.

"What do you mean you had to?" I needed details, but at the same time I didn't want them. I was angry, tired, and sick all at once. Now I wanted Chase to be dead. Lucky for him, he was.

"Candice, please. It's not what you think. We were undercover. If we hadn't, we could have been killed. The case we were working on was in trafficking. They wanted me tried out, so to speak, before making a purchase. Chase tried to get us out of it, but instead of letting them rape me, he took the challenge and saved both our lives."

It sounded noble, but I was still sick. My dead fiancé was having a baby with my best friend. They didn't make up drama this good on *Days of our Lives*. I rolled my eyes and silently made a wish on the water pouring from the clouds that the night would end.

"Candice, he saved my life and the cost is to have his baby. We were going to deal with it, but his mom found out. She begged me to let her have her if I wouldn't raise her myself."

Tears rolled down her face as if she were pleading for her life. I should be angry, but I was too tired and my emotional rollercoaster was coming to an end for the day. A girl can only endure so much before she has to call it all to a halt. I was at my breaking point again. I needed this drama away from me.

"Christina, we will talk about this later, when I am not so angry. I need you to leave now. I want some space."

Jax refused to let me up. I watched Christina rise and head for the door. She didn't turn to look back at me, which was probably for the best. She'd held this secret for months. Couldn't she have held it in a little longer, or even lied about who the father was? My Chase had cheated on me, for work, or for whatever reason. *He* should have been the one to tell me.

Chapter Six

I chose to sleep in the guest room that night where there were no photos of Chase. It was plain and empty so I didn't have to worry about seeing anything that would flash a memory and break my heart all over again.

Jax slept beside me in the guest bed all night. Entangled in each other for comfort and warmth. It was the best night's sleep I'd had since I learned of Chase's death. I peeked up at the alarm clock, which sat on the black nightstand beside the four poster bed.

I still had a couple hours before sunrise and my head was swimming with things I didn't want to think about. I turned to face Jax, who smiled at me. This was exactly what I needed.

I had spent the last few months wondering why Chase kept sleeping on the couch. I wondered what I had done wrong, thinking he didn't want to hold me or touch me. I wondered if it was because he worked so much, or if we were going to turn into one of those couples who scheduled our sex twice a year.

The winds flowed through the house, causing the smoke colored curtains to flutter. The thunder cracked in the distance and I embraced the sound. I scooted closer to Jax as I pulled up the comforter.

"Can't sleep?" he asked as the winds howled.

"My body put it to a vote and it said no more sleeping. Apparently my insomnia vetoed the law my head tried to pass to allow for at least three hours of sleep a day."

Jax smiled at my poorly worded joke, as the lightning lit up the sky behind him. I loved a storm when the seasons were fighting for territory. They were always loud, sometimes severe, but more importantly it brought my raindrop wishes.

"Jax, sing me a song."

Jax had a beautiful singing voice. When he went to the bar and sang karaoke, the women would swoon at his tenor notes. As Jax began singing, my heart melted. This man had a gift that left me in awe.

He pulled the comforter up over my shoulder as I stared into his eyes. The lightning in the background was a perfect addition to the moment, as if the world was in sync with us. Jax had picked the perfect song, my favorite: "So Far Away" by Avenged Sevenfold.

I listened as he sang the first verse perfectly. I had heard the song a million times, but with everything that had happened recently, it took on a new meaning and pulled right at my heart strings.

The thunder rolled in tune with Jax, and the lightning cracked. The rain pounded heavily on the roof. The wind carried rain through the window and let it pool on the floor. I was involved in an orchestra of events that made me see things differently at that moment.

Jax continued singing and I cuddled against his body. We were chest to chest as my face rested near his neck. I tugged on his thigh and placed it over my leg, which I slid in between his thighs. I rubbed my hands up and down his chiseled back as he serenaded my soul.

As he sang and the weather joined in the chorus, I made a wish on the raindrops that splattered far enough across the room to land on my cheek. I wished that this moment of friendship was enough to help us both heal. I wished that I would let go of the bitterness I felt toward Chase. I hoped my wish carried my hope that Jax would not feel guilt from losing his partner and best friend. I wished this moment would stay perfect in my memory.

As Jax came to the last chorus, I looked into his gray eyes which seemed to carry soft strands of light blue in his irises. His tanned skin glistened as the rain pattered near the bed. Neither of us moved to close the window because then, this moment would be broken.

I stared at his thinned lips as his smile dissipated. A raindrop flew in and landed on his face, splashing against his lip. I placed my lips on the drop of water, and there was a fleeting moment in which our lips touched, but it was like sparks of electricity flew from our veins.

I pulled back and looked at Jax who didn't seem to move. I leaned back and placed my lips on his. They felt like hot velvet. I moved my arm up and gripped the back of his neck. Jax slid his sultry tongue across my lips and I opened for his entry.

After months of being ignored, and learning that Chase had cheated, I needed the passion. I needed to feel wanted. I wanted to feel needed. More importantly, I needed to feel loved. I couldn't have that with Chase because he was gone. I would always be sour with the way he left things unsaid, but here and now in this moment Chase was not who I was thinking about.

Jax's arm slid under the comforter and wrapped around my back, pulling me sharply into him. I let out a light groan of need as he pulled back to look breathlessly at me.

"I don't want you to do anything you might regret," he whispered. I tilted my body to lay on my back and pulled on his necklace until he was on top of me.

"Ditto." I spoke softly as I looked up into his eyes which pierced my soul to tell me he was safe.

"Candice, I could never regret being with you in any way."

Jax leaned down and placed his warm, wet lips on mine and I opened to devour the rush of mint that came with his tongue. He must not have slept at all because I could still smell his toothpaste and tasted his mouthwash as if he had just used them. The more we kissed, the stronger the smell of Irish Spring invaded my nose and made me crave more.

"You taste like strawberries," Jax whispered as he tried to catch his breath.

"Lip gloss," I replied as I pulled on his boxers. Once they were off, I reached for his long length, but he pulled himself out of my reach. He leaned up and kissed my neck. I turned, giving him more space as I was unable to resist him. I felt him pull down my boy shorts and goosebumps broke out across my skin.

Next he took off my tank top and we were both naked, looking at each other as the storm raged on outside the window and inside our broken hearts.

Jax kissed me slowly and softly, smoothing his tongue across my lips, which parted immediately as if I had been trained to let him in. He pinned my hands above my head and used his knee to spread my legs. He moved from my lips to my neck as I squirmed in reaction.

"God, Candice, you are so beautiful. You are better than a fantasy."

He moved from my neck to stare at my ample breasts. My nipples hardened as he flicked his tongue out. At the first lick, my back arched off the bed as I instinctively tried to slip my nipple back inside his mouth.

My hips undulated under him as he sucked my nipple back into his mouth. I moaned with need as the rain splashed on my face, adding to the intimacy of the moment.

Jax released my hands as he made a path down my abdomen, stopping to kiss every inch in his path down to the apex between my legs. I held my breath as I waited, as his face was now at the center of my raging hormones. I felt my heart pulsing in my clit as he blew a soft release of air from his mouth onto my bare mound.

"God, please..." I cried out. Jax smiled up at me as he spread my folds with his fingers.

"Do you want me here?" He slid one finger over the tight bundle of pulsating nerves.

"Yes, God yes." I cried out as the thunder crashed over the house. I swore it vibrated the bed as Jax swiped his tongue across my clit. I could feel my wetness stream as he continued his onslaught.

"I could do this all night. You taste so sweet and tangy," he whispered before his tongue found its way to my entrance.

"Yes," I seethed through my teeth. My toes curled and my breasts felt heavy as I gripped the bed sheet in my fists. My moans mingled with the thunder that rumbled. My heart raced, and my breathing grew erratic as Jax slid one finger inside me. Sweat broke out across my body as a rush of heat rolled through me when he sucked my clit into his mouth, while finding that rough patch inside me with his finger.

"Jax," I called out, and he glanced up.

"You rang?" he said, grinning, and I pushed his head back between my legs. I gasped the second my clit was sucked back into his mouth. He released it and his tongue graced my clit in a relaxed pace as if we were going to be there all night.

I could feel the orgasm welling up inside me, so strong. I curled my toes and grabbed his hair as I climbed the cliff that I would surely fall off of.

My stomach tightened, my nipples hardening. My skin flourished as my body turned rosy. I gritted my teeth and clamped down on his finger as my body burst into a thousand different directions. The first wave stole my breath as he continued his languid licking of my clit.

"Jax," I screamed as I found my breath, and the second wave carried away my fears. He pulled his fingers out of me and I whimpered as my clit continued to pulse with unleashed waves that needed to flow.

I watched as he rose up and climbed up my tight body with kisses here and there as he moved toward me. When he pressed his lips on mine, I tasted mint mixed with my own flavor—intoxicatingly delicious.

I forced him to deepen his kiss, grasping the back of his neck, hoping he would impale me on his cock, which was poised at my entrance. He slowly moved forward with small strides to pull back every so often. It was a tease as my pussy wall vibrated with that unrelenting need to hold him inside me. He continued his softened pace until I was breathless and full.

"You all right?" Jax asked as my eyes glistened from the wave of intense intimacy that was transpiring. No one had ever been inside me but Chase, and my heart was pouring out sadness to make room for whatever this was.

"I feel like a sexy, emotional popsicle."

"No one can ever say you don't have a way with words. I don't think I will ever hear those words together in a sentence again," Jax stated with a smile as he stayed completely still inside me. He brushed my hair away from my face. "Do you want me to stop?" he whispered.

"No."

He began slow movements in and out of me, interlocking our fingers. He placed them down on the bed and held them there while he found his rhythm. I curled my legs around his waist to get him deeper inside me.

The storm had softened, but the thunder said it wasn't done yet, and neither were we. Jax let go of my hands and moved them to my hips. He sat up and lifted me just a hair off the bed. It was enough for him to rub that spot again and again.

When he laid me back down, I was so swollen, I could feel all of him, everywhere. I felt a rapid stirring in my loins as he drove into me a little faster.

"You are so tight and wet. You're going to kill me," Jax muttered as he came down to kiss my neck. I would surely wear a hickey tomorrow, but I didn't care. I was enthralled. As he bit down lightly on my neck, I tightened on his cock and heard his groan.

The winds picked up and rain poured in the open window onto us, as our bodies reached a climax. I clamped down even tighter on Jax and watched as he gritted his teeth and pushed harder into me. The orgasm rumbled like thunder and cracked like lightning, through me and into Jax.

"Chase," I screamed out without thinking, as Jax simultaneously shouted, "Candy."

I closed my eyes as he came to a stop, hoping he didn't hear me call out Chase's name. In my release, my heartache and sorrow fled with it. I could still feel my broken heart, but the ache wasn't as bad as the guilt I now felt. The guilt grew as added feelings about what we had just done manifested within seconds and I wanted to flee. I opened my eyes to see the hurt on his face. There was no denying he had heard me.

"Jax..."

What was there to say? I could apologize for calling him by my fiancé's name, but I felt like that wouldn't be enough. It suddenly seemed like our friendship had just taken a turn into the twilight zone.

Jax pulled out of me and I immediately missed him. I watched without words as he grabbed his boxers and put them back on. He stood up and walked to the window and closed it. Shutting me out from the storm.

"Jax." I spoke softly as I pulled the comforter up.

"Get some sleep. We will talk about it in the morning." He leaned over and gave me a kiss on my forehead. I suddenly felt alone. My emotional dam burst, and I cried into the pillow as Jax left the room. I was broken and this time I had no one to lean on. I had done this to myself. I had broken our friendship.

I let myself cry it out, and then got up and donned a black bra and underwear, and put on my over-sized Metallica hoody over my skinny jeans. I walked through the puddle and opened the window to let the storm soothe me. Then I put everything back in my suitcase and zipped it up.

I knew I had to leave, but saying goodbye would be too hard. I rummaged through his nightstand and found a piece of paper and a pen. I sat and wrote Jax a note. He deserved so much more than a letter, but I am a coward. I left the letter on the bed and stood to get my things ready. I was going to take what I could and go out the window to avoid hurting him any further.

I heard something at the door and watched as an envelope slid across the floor. I stared at the envelope as if it taunted me with more heartache. In the back of my mind I pretended Jax had written me a note, but I knew that was not what was in the envelope. My next heartache was sitting there, sealed with tape.

I picked it up off the floor. I read how the cover was addressed, and hugged it to my chest. It read *In Case of my Death*. I don't know what was worse, the way he left and the things he had done, or the fact that the letter was dated two days before he died. I slid to the floor as my heart sunk.

This was Chase saying goodbye. I had been hurt that he died, furious he had not told me about Christina, but as I held this envelope, I was empty.

When Chase died, I think he took everything I had in me with him. What little bit of me was left went with Jax when I let him inside me. I was a hollow shell of a woman left to pick herself up and move on alone. I prepared my heart, opened the letter, and began to read it.

Candice,

If you are reading this, then I wasn't the big bad superhero I always thought I was. I never had any intention of leaving you alone in this life. I wanted you with me until the very end, and the thing is I did have you until my very end. I hope you won't mind me looking down on you from Heaven. I know it's supposed to be a glorious place and I will be at peace there, but my heart will still be on Earth with you.

I made so many mistakes in my life, and one of them was never trusting you with all of me. I learned I am going to have a daughter with Christina. I am sure the news is clearly devastating, considering I didn't tell you. I never wanted anyone but you. I didn't want a baby with Christina, but when the time came to choose, I chose life In that choice, I created one. I knew if I told you I might lose you, and I wasn't willing to take that risk. I would have rather spent every day with you happy than to watch you in pain from the actions I took Be angry with me, not with anyone else. I have earned your wrath, so if you want to spit on my grave, it's okay. I understand.

I am sad that I have left you, but I know you will be okay. Jaxson loves you more than life itself. You love him, too, even if you don't see it now, you will. Give yourself time to heal I am sure he will wait for you. I couldn't think of a better man to ask to take care of you while I am gone than one that loves you so completely. I want you and Jaxson to take care of each other as if I had never been there. Lean on each other in times of need, hold each other in times of sorrow, and laugh together in times of joy.

Don't let my death affect you so deeply that you never move on Don't let my betrayal of your trust lead you down a darkened path where you stop trusting everyone. Give your dad a chance to know you. He wants to; he just doesn't know how. Live your life like every day is your last, because when my last day came I had no regrets other than I would never be able to give you a good with the bad kiss goodbye.

I will love you forever and always,

Chase

Chapter Seven

Seven months later...

I awoke to my alarm clock going off at five in the morning. It was time for work. I had, once upon a time, been a best-selling author. Now I was a cubical junkie for a computer company. After moving and leaving everything behind, I needed the change. I loved my job, which kept me busy and entertained. The water cooler comments alone could write their own book. It was always *did you know she was doing this with... with her... while they... under him... oh, you know she liked it*. It was a regular soap opera in there.

I stretched as I rolled out of bed. The time difference between east coast and west coast made it feel as though I was sleeping in every single day. I placed my perfectly pedicured toes onto the bare hardwood floor, which was always cold in the morning as I walked to the shower.

I had found a two-bedroom house outside of Los Angeles. I could not deal with being in the city because the traffic was awful. I thought New York City traffic was bad. Nope, Los Angeles had it beat.

I walked into the bathroom and opened the glass door to turn on the shower. I stripped out of my pajamas as I waited for the water to heat, staring at the shadow box that held a freeze-dried four-leaf clover and a red rose petal on my wall. It was all I had from home. I had everything else sent to the dump since it had been damaged from the break-in.

I had been told not to make any serious changes for one year. They say it's a time for grieving, but I was sinking and had to make some very real changes or I would have drowned. I had placed the house on the market a couple of days ago, thinking I was finally in a good place emotionally. No one knew me here, or had any real expectations of me. I thought about Jax and missed his friendship from time to time, but I think the friendship ended when I left. Plus, I had made friends here as well. I worked hard to forget him and that part of my life.

I stepped into the shower and began to wash my hair when I heard the phone ring. A familiar tune meant my boss, Andrew, was calling. He had been calling every morning for the last three months to make sure I was up, offering to carpool, and even providing breakfast. I was quickly growing to love my boss. He'd been the temporary replacement after my first boss was killed in a hit-and-run, so I worried he would be transferred any day.

I never had a boss who saw me every day before, but if everyone's boss was this great I couldn't see why anyone complained. Andrew was the best. It was a thirty-minute ride just to get into the city, so four of us met every morning at my house and he drove us through the horrid traffic on the 405.

I finished showering and stepped out to hear a knock at my door. I quickly threw my hair up in a towel and fastened my black satin robe. I could smell the coffee before I even opened the door. I knew it was Andrew.

"Hi, Andrew, how are you this morning?" I smiled, reaching for the bag he'd brought to see what delicious treat I was getting today. For a moment, I had a weird thought that I was a dog who got a treat whenever she did something good. I had to shake the idea from my mind.

"Hello, gorgeous, do you always answer the door wearing nothing but a robe when a man brings you food?" He spoke with laughter in his voice, his green eyes dancing in delight when he saw my excitement. He took the bag from my hands since I was fumbling to get it open.

"What do I get today?" I asked, clapping my hands like a toddler. I was so excited to bond with him this way. It had nothing to do with breakfast, but more about him being a great friend. I was short a few best friends, but Andrew was climbing his way into one of those spots.

He headed into my kitchen, which was composed of an oven, a refrigerator, and three white bottom cabinets. I had a small pantry, but I used it to store pots and pans instead of food. I had never been much of a cook, so the yellow and white kitchen, which was more Barbie-sized rather than life-sized, did not bother me.

I watched as he hunted for something, and then figured out he was going to cook when I saw the carton of eggs sticking out of the bag. I went to the pantry, but the door stuck as I pulled on the handle. Andrew came up behind me to help as the door swung open and I plowed backward into him.

"Are you okay?" I asked, peeling us both off the floor. My cheeks turned crimson with embarrassment when I realized my robe had untied itself. Although, I could have sworn I double-knotted it.

"I know I make your place look good, but do you really want me to be part of your décor so bad that you would implant me in the wall?"

He smiled at me as he took off his jacket and placed it on the card table I used for a dining room table. He un-cuffed his button-down shirt and rolled up his sleeves as if to get to work. After smiling at the way he was dancing around my kitchen, I left the room to finish dressing.

My long brown hair was showing curls again, and I would have to straighten it before I showed my face anywhere outside the bathroom. As I set about straightening my hair, I smelled bacon and my mouth began to water. Who didn't love bacon?

I quickly finished my hair and applied minimal make-up. I walked out of the bathroom and headed straight for the closet in my bedroom, where I slid open the bi-fold doors and stared ahead at my clothes. They were in color order by season and size, because I had nothing else to do in my downtime other than organize my closet. I grabbed a black pencil skirt, then a white button-down shirt and a pair of black heels that wrapped around my ankles.

I laid the clothes out on the bed as the aroma from the kitchen made my stomach clench with hunger. Grabbing a black lace bra with matching panties and a garter along with a pair of thigh-highs, I proceeded to get dressed.

Some mornings I really did miss writing my novels. The characters liked to scream out in my head that they needed to be heard, but I still had nothing to say. I missed creating those characters who knew what they were doing with their lives and everyone lived happily ever after, but that was the past and it needed to stay behind me. I had to focus and move forward.

I checked myself in the mirror and flattened my hands over my skirt to make sure it was straight. I grabbed my purse off the nightstand that sat across from my four poster mahogany bed. I turned out the light and headed to the kitchen.

"Andrew, you should just move in and be my personal chef," I uttered with a groan, as the now sweetened smell mixed with a hint of cinnamon. I heard laughter as I entered the kitchen.

"Darling girl, you could not afford to keep me!"

I smiled at the intended joke, even if I did not really follow it. I grabbed my cup of Tim Hortons' coffee. There were no Tim Hortons where we lived, as the majority of them are in the north, but after living in New York all those years it was the one addiction I missed the most. I still had the noise and traffic by living near a large city, but the coffee was the one thing I had every morning with Chase and Jax. My stomach was the only part of me that I would allow to miss home.

I closed my eyes and poured it into my mouth, savoring the flavor. Andrew's parents lived in Buffalo, New York and shipped him the Tim Hortons coffee grounds weekly. I think he had enough to live off coffee the rest of our days and then some.

I opened the front door and walked down the one step to the short pathway to the mailbox. I grabbed the newspapers and brought them inside, placing the Los Angeles Times where Andrew always sat. I took a seat and opened the New York Times. As I started reading, I heard him clear his throat. Looking up from the paper, I smiled when I saw Andrew holding two plates.

"My darling girl, why do you read east coast news when you live on the west coast?"

Andrew set the plate down in front of me before I could answer. The strawberry and banana stuffed French toast was topped with fresh cut fruit. The scrambled eggs had little bits of bacon cooked inside. I reached for the extra bacon strips Andrew had put on the side. This man could be a dream for whoever eventually nabbed him.

"Mmmm, this is delicious," I uttered, my mouth full of bacon. The common courtesy of not talking with your mouth full went out the window when the food melted in your mouth. My taste buds danced in excitement with each bite. I would gain a thousand pounds if Andrew cooked all my food.

My phone chimed with a reminder that it was nearly six. The rest of the carpool would be here soon. I shoveled as much food into my mouth as I could and grabbed my paper to get my fix. Andrew sat across from me reading his Los Angeles Times. It was all very domesticated. I still did not understand why people did not love their bosses.

At fifteen minutes after six, my doorbell rang and Andrew leaped into action to answer it. Emily was a beautiful blonde with legs up to her chest. She had that innocent look about her. She did not have to work, as her parents owned a candy company, but she desperately wanted to prove she did not need things handed to her. I admired that about her.

"Hi, Emily. How are you this morning?" I asked, offering a drink by waving my hand toward the kitchen table, where Andrew had placed freshly squeezed orange juice.

"It is morning," Emily replied flatly, with Andrew laughing in response.

"My two best employees are polar opposites. One is a morning person and indulges me with sharing breakfast, while the other parties all night and graces me with a grumpy face until lunch." He shook his head as he began loading the dishwasher.

"Where is Brent?" I asked, as he was usually the first one to arrive.

"He is driving in today. He has to get his car fixed during lunch and the mechanic is three blocks from the office," Andrew replied as he unrolled his sleeves and we all prepared to leave.

Emily was pouring a cup of orange juice into one of my travel mugs. I grabbed my phone and placed it in my purse, double checking that I had my keys and ID inside as well. I saw that Chase's letter had crinkled at the bottom, so I pulled it out, folding it before placing it back inside the zipper portion inside my black Calvin Klein purse. I did not know what the appropriate course of action was with letters like that, but I liked carrying it with me. It was a reminder of how short life was and how badly one person could hurt another. It was my personal reminder that kept me from forgetting the past and reminding me that the future couldn't guarantee people I loved would always be there.

As I draped my purse across my forearm, my phone rang, an unfamiliar tone. I pulled it out and opened the wallet case to see a New York area code. Closing my eyes, secretly wishing it was Jax so I could apologize, I answered. I had never apologized to him; I didn't have the courage.

"Hello?"

"Hello, I am trying to reach a Candice-Leigh Carson." A feminine voice came across the line, her tone friendly yet stern.

"This is she."

"Ms. Carson, my name is Brooklyn Montgomery. I am the A.D.A. here in New York County. I wondered if you had a moment to speak to me."

My heart dropped. I do not know why people say they want justice, because when justice calls, the voice on the other line either gives you good news or bad and it brings it all back to the surface again.

I turned away from everyone and walked into the living room. I didn't want anyone to hear my conversation even though my house was matchbox-sized and I knew they would.

"Yes, Ms. Montgomery, I have the time now," I replied with a shaky breath.

"Ms. Carson, please call me Brooklyn. I would like for you to feel comfortable talking to me."

I nodded as if she could see me. Thankfully, she continued on as I swallowed hard. This was not how I wanted to spend a Monday morning.

"Ms. Carson, we have a suspect for the break-in at your home. I wondered if you would have time to go and talk with a detective there in Los Angeles or if you would be returning to New York anytime soon?"

"I can make the time to talk to a detective here. I have no intentions of returning to New York."

"All right, I will call you back when I determine who will be handling this out there on your end. One last thing, Ms. Carson: when was your last communication with Detective Jaxson Monroe?"

"I haven't spoken to Jaxson in six months or more. I left a couple weeks after the funeral," I stated as I closed my eyes and thought about what Jax would have felt when he awoke to a letter on the bed and me gone. I didn't want that life following me so while I wished that Jax would call, I had changed my number so he couldn't. "Why do you ask?" I added, closing my eyes as if it would protect my heart.

"He took a temporary leave of absence and I was just checking in on him. If you have not spoken to him, then I will try to reach his girlfriend again."

I felt as though I could vomit. The word girlfriend was running through my mind on a big flashing banner. I don't know why I was so upset, but I could not speak. A tear streamed down my cheek.

"Ms. Carson, I know this is hard for you, but we are doing our best to determine who broke into your house and who killed your fiancé. I am not on your fiancé's case, but if I can help in any way please let me know."

I sniffled, trying to dry up my tears. Brooklyn must have heard me. I had people in the house with me and yet I felt alone.

"Ms. Carson, I truly am sorry for your loss. I will be in touch with the contact information for the PD there. The number on your caller ID is my cell. You can reach me anytime."

Just like that, the call ended and my world tilted once again. I dropped my phone into my purse and covered my face as I began to sob. I thought I was fine. I thought I was beyond this, but nearly seven months later it is day one all over again. Jax had moved on, so why couldn't I?

Andrew walked into the room and wrapped his long arms around me. I felt nothing. No warmth, no comfort. I was numb to the world around me. I pulled away and gave both Andrew and Emily, who was now in the archway, the best smile I could before I walked to the bathroom.

I closed the door and wiped my tears. I washed my face and wiped it dry. I saw my reflection in the mirror, my puffy red eyes screaming defeat. My pale skin was inflamed with red blotches, almost as if I was blushing. It happened whenever I got upset. I cleared my throat and applied new make-up to look the best I could. A knock on the door made me jump. I opened it to see Andrew.

"Want to talk?" he asked sweetly.

"It was a long time ago."

"Who is Jaxson?" He spoke softly as he leaned in my doorframe.

"He used to be a friend."

"Used to be? Want to tell me what happened?"

I stood silently, placing my hands on the sink and staring at myself. I had to forgive Chase, and the person who killed him, in order to keep my sanity. I also needed to accept my responsibility for the way I bolted on Jax.

"Jax was my fiancé's partner. I let things go too far one night and, because I did not want to face him, I climbed out his guest bedroom window, climbed down his garden trellis, and fled to the airport to come here. I haven't spoken to him since."

"Candice, obviously the mention of this man upsets you. Don't you think maybe you should find him and apologize? It might help you move on as well." Andrew stepped away a moment later, closing the bathroom door behind him.

Bringing up Jax was like putting the nail in my coffin. I only wanted what was best for him and I was not it. An apology was nowhere close to what that man deserved, and I was too ashamed to grovel.

The conversation with Brooklyn threw me off. He had a girlfriend now? It didn't seem to fit the Jax I knew. I should have spoken up and said something, but I did not have the courage to see him or apologize, so it wasn't right for me to ask about him.

Chapter Eight

The day passed by in a blur. It was nearly time to leave and I had been taking calls all day about a new anti-virus program our company had released. Everyone had questions which I had to research the answers to, because we had been late and weren't briefed this morning. The added time to figure out the answers kept me busy. I missed lunch, but it was all right because I wasn't hungry.

I checked my emails on the computer to see a lot of messages from Emily, who wanted to see if I was okay. I deleted them all and grabbed my purse, shutting down the computer for the day. I patted the side of my purse where Chase's letter was, grabbed my coat, and headed for the elevator.

I saw Andrew in his office pacing while on the phone. He looked agitated, which was outside of the norm for him. I wondered what was going on. I pushed the elevator button, and held my gaze to his. He smiled at me and gave me a wink. I smiled back, feeling reassured that everything would be okay.

We had taken Andrew's car this morning, but I had a key. After going down twenty stories, I walked up to his silver Mercedes. I thought I heard thunder. Outside the parking garage, I noticed the clouds were covering the sun, but there was no storm on the horizon for me.

My body shivered as fall had turned to winter and those rumors about California always being eighty degrees and sunny were a lie. They said on the news we were expecting a rare thunderstorm, with lightning and hail. I went back to the car and used my key to get inside and wait for Andrew to drive me home.

I thought about Jax and wondered what he was doing. The word *girlfriend* had been swarming my thoughts all day. I wasn't sure what it was that didn't sit right with me, but he was no longer mine to hold. I had made a huge mistake the last time I saw him.

He always had a place in my heart, but making love to him was a mistake. I had hurt him by calling out Chase's name. I was already grieving; the added guilt from my actions were too much to take.

I had left a note on the bed, stored my luggage in his closet, and snuck out of the second story window. I got a flight and was halfway to California before he woke up to talk to me. When I landed in Los Angeles, I checked my messages to see he had called me over a hundred times. I thanked him for being a friend by changing my number and never returning his calls.

"Hey, darling," Andrew said, pulling me from my thoughts. "Would you like to grab dinner with me tonight?"

I nodded my approval and we headed out to eat before going home for the night.

Dinner had been a delight. Andrew took me to a top-rated restaurant in Los Angeles, my first time having Japanese food.

"Candice, we need to talk," he said as we left.

"I detest when people say that," I muttered and then put my hand over my mouth at the realization I had said it out loud. I pulled my hand down and flushed with embarrassment; word vomit typically had that effect. "I am so sorry, Andrew. What is it we need to talk about?"

"You have been picked to go with me to our corporate retreat next week."

I was elated because I hadn't been there very long, but I had worked my butt off to be recognized for the work I did. It seemed someone had taken notice.

"What do we have to do?" I asked.

"We will take the rest of the week getting our charts made to show how our products are improving over the rest. Then we fly to New York and present them to the people who give us paychecks."

Andrew unlocked the car and held the door open for me as the realization of returning to New York sank in. After we were both in the car, I couldn't think of a single thing to say other than *no*. I wasn't ready to go back there.

"Andrew, can't Emily go in my place?" I said as he finally pulled up at my house.

"Candice, tell me what the problem is and maybe I can help."

I took a deep breath and thought about it. I could tell him everything about Jax and my dad, but were they valid reasons not to go for work? I invited him inside. Within minutes of walking into the house, Andrew was brewing coffee and I went to get into my pajamas to relax.

I dressed in fuzzy pink plaid pajama pants and a white tank top and piled my hair in a messy bun. I resurfaced in the living room where Andrew was waiting with a hot decaf coffee for me. He sat on the couch and I sat down beside him.

"I left a mess behind back in New York." I spoke softly and then blew on my coffee. I saw that I had Andrew's undivided attention and decided to let him in. "Remember earlier when you asked about Jax? My fiancé died, after knocking up someone who used to be one of my best friends. Then I took an opening and slept with my dead fiancé's partner, Jax. I left a note, snuck out of his window, and changed my phone number."

"Is that all?" Andrew asked, and I felt relief that he wasn't judging me for my choices.

"My dad is there too, but I have barely spoken to him since my mom died," I whispered and then sipped my coffee. "I love my dad, and want to see him, but the rift between us is deeper than the ocean."

"Candice." Andrew took my hand in his. "There are almost nine million people in the Big Apple. What makes you think that you would see any of those people? You will be working the whole time and will barely leave the hotel. I think you are making this too big of a deal. Ask yourself: is it that you are afraid to run into these people, or do you want to run into them, but are afraid of what you will find?"

I would take the time to think about it, but asking me a question like that while holding my hand made me think that since I was being honest about it now, there was no way to even fake being sick to get out of this one.

My stomach turned and I breathed through the nausea. Going back to a place I could no longer call home was inevitable. Maybe it was time I took Jax's advice about ripping it off like a Band-Aid, and just went.

I leaned over and curled into Andrew and he wrapped his arms around me.

"You know, Candice, not many bosses are this nice."

I looked up at Andrew, who had a huge grin on his face.

"What is it you want?" I asked as I snuggled against him, "and how much will it cost me?"

"When we go to New York, I would like you to accompany me as my date to dinner at The View," Andrew whispered as he leaned down and kissed my forehead. I shifted my body without a word spoken and laid my head in his lap. I looked up into his green eyes which danced in the light. His eyes were not like Chase's, which had spoken about his character. Andrew's eyes were not like Jaxson's; his spoke of comfort and warmth. Andrew's green eyes merely showed kindness when he looked at me.

"Are you sure you're not gay?" I asked with a smirk.

"I think I would know," Andrew replied as he sipped his coffee above me. "Why would you ask?"

"I was thinking how great my life would be if I had a gay best friend. Then I wouldn't have to worry about when my robe flies open. I could just walk around naked."

Andrew nearly spit his coffee out with laughter.

"That is the highlight of my mornings. You can't take that away," Andrew stated with a puckered lip and sad puppy eyes. He looked pitiful.

"You keep cooking for me like you do, and there will be a whole lot of woman to see," I replied with a smile.

"'Tis my job to serve you, M'lady," Andrew stated as he bowed his head.

"You're insufferable," I said with a giggle.

"You love me," Andrew replied and smiled down at me. This was nice. This was what I used to have with Chase before he passed away.

Andrew and I finished our coffee with laughter and stories on why the west coast is better than the east. He left a short time later, and I pulled out my laptop. I booted it up and looked up Facebook. I had removed my account when I changed my number and even changed my email, too.

I essentially cut all of New York out of my life. I started a new account with a photo of another girl I stole off Google, and then proceeded to look for Jax and Christina's pages.

I found Christina's first. It showed her hugging her ready-to-pop pregnant belly while she stood next to Chase's mom. Time said she'd had the baby, but I was grateful I didn't have to see the evidence of what her and Chase had done. I wanted to punch the screen. I think it was safe to say my bitterness did not dissipate with distance or time.

Then I found Jax. He had a photo of himself in his dress policeman's uniform with a blonde on his arm. Jax didn't like blondes. As long as I had known him, he had been partial to brunettes. She was in three more pictures, hanging on him. There was one photo where she was pulling on his St. Michael necklace to kiss him.

I balled my fist with a new rush of anger. I had given him that necklace when Chase died. Michael was the patron saint for police officers; I made him wear it to stay safe. There she was using it to stick her tongue down his throat. *No telling where that tongue has been.*

I slammed the lid on my laptop and went to bed. I tossed and turned thinking about what Jax would be doing right now. I groaned when my brain responded with the thought that he was *doing* her. I don't know why I was so angry. It wasn't as if Jax was mine. I belonged to Chase.

At that moment it sunk in that I belonged to no one. Chase would always have a piece of my heart, but I had nothing. If I wanted to die a shriveled up old woman all alone then I was on the right path, but I still wanted kids and I wanted to be able to share my life with someone.

I glanced at the clock. It was two in the morning and still I could not sleep. I had vivid images of Chase, Jax, Christina, and the unnamed blonde Barbie with big boobs and a flat stomach rolling through my head. I couldn't take it anymore. I grabbed my phone and called my voicemail.

Inside the menu, it allows me to put in a number and leave a message where I don't have to call and wake anyone up. The first person I left a voicemail for was Andrew and I told him I would go to New York, but wanted a day off to clear my head prior to leaving.

The second voicemail I left was for Jax. I sat in silence when the beep came. My anger spurred onward, but my head said I was being jealous and it would pass. As I sat in silence on the line, the seconds ticked onward. I thought about all the things I could say. Then I said the only thing that came to mind.

"I don't know why I called. I'm sorry."

Then I hung up the phone. He had obviously moved on with his life, and I was still holding on to a dead man. It had been months since I laid Chase in the ground, but I had picked myself up and dusted myself off since then. I'd made something of myself despite the constant feeling that I was disappointing Chase. I could look past the cheating part because we had twenty years of memories that said that he was a great man, even if he had hurt me.

I grabbed my phone and placed a third voicemail. I called Chase's mom, Michelle.

"Hi, Michelle, it's me. I know you are probably angry that I bailed and left you to grieve alone. I thought I owed you an explanation as to why I left. So here it is. I am a heartbroken coward who can't help anyone else if I can't help myself. I have thought about you every day. I wonder how you're doing all the time. I hope the baby helps fill the gap in your heart that Chase's death left in everyone. Most of all I hope you find peace with this. You will always be my second mom, even if I am no longer your daughter. I love you."

I hung up, shedding a tear. I should call my dad and let him know I would be in New York. We didn't really speak, but Chase's letter asked that I give him a chance and I was going to honor Chase's last words. I closed my phone again. I would call him closer to the trip.

I decided to start pulling up the percentages for the charts, since my brain was not going to let me sleep anyway. I began the research needed for each of the talking points Andrew had mentioned. It would be easier if I had a list of everything, but this was a starting point and I had nothing else to do.

Hours flew by and soon my phone was ringing to tell me Andrew was on his way. I put my laptop down beside my phone on the coffee table and jumped in the shower.

Within twenty minutes, Andrew was looking over the work I had done while we ate croissants that had bacon, egg, and cheese inside of them.

"These are great," Andrew said with a smile. "When did you sleep last night?"

"I didn't. My body refused to let me," I replied.

"Take the day off and get some rest. You have done more than enough work for the day. I will email you a list of everything else we need in case your insomnia lasts more than a day."

Just like that, he was gone with Emily and Brent on their carpool to work. In the beige bathroom, I ran a hot bubble bath in the large garden tub. The bathroom was the entire reason I decided this house would be good for me.

I turned on the music player on my phone and placed it on the white and cream marbled sink as I climbed inside. As I laid in the tub, my body finally relaxed and I started drifting off to sleep. I woke up to my phone ringing an unfamiliar song, and chilled water.

I got out of the tub, thankful I hadn't drowned, and wrapped a towel around my body. In the bedroom, I slipped into a pair of sweats and a tank top.

I grabbed my phone and headed back into the living room. There were a few messages from Andrew telling me we would be leaving in ten days, along with a list of what we needed. There was also a voicemail from an unlisted number. I called and listened and nearly dropped the phone when I heard Jax's voice come through.

"I'm always here if you need me."

Chapter Nine

The days had flown by. How could it be Thursday already? I had just gotten back from getting my hair ombre'd from brown to blonde and was packing my bag as quick as I could. Our flight was in just a few hours. I hadn't heard another word from Jax, but I made no attempt to call him either. Instead, I listened to his message a million times.

I stalked his social media as more photos of the blonde showed up. I must be a glutton for punishment. As much as it bothered me, I kept looking to see if she was still in the picture. I couldn't shake the unnatural hatred I felt for her without even knowing her. I really should have stopped looking, but I had become a cyber-stalker and could no longer help myself.

After packing my bags, I set them by the front door and walked into the living room with my phone. I wanted to call my dad and check on him. When my mom died, he didn't know how to cope with it or how to raise me on his own, so we stopped talking, and Chase's mom and Jax's parents stepped in and helped. Jax and Chase spent so much time with my dad that it allowed me to maintain my distance from him.

I was never angry with him for how things turned out. I hoped that we would fall into a better relationship one day, but it hadn't happened. My birthday was on Saturday and we would be in New York, so I wanted to see if my dad wanted to go out to celebrate the big twenty-five.

"Hey, Daddy." I spoke softly when he answered the phone.

"Hey, Candy it has been a while, how have you been?"

"I am good, Dad, how are you?" I asked as I paced the floor.

"I'm good, Candy Cane. I miss seeing your face around here." His reply tugged at my heart.

"Dad, I am coming into town for work. We'll be here for a week. Do you want to go to dinner with me Saturday night?"

"For your birthday? Of course, but wouldn't you rather spend the time with your friends?" My dad had no idea what had transpired to make me leave, and obviously no one had told him.

"No, I was thinking we could grab something from Gray's Papaya or the Cafeteria."

"I'm in. I love both places and would love to see you. How is California?"

"It's good. Surprisingly cold, but good. How is everything at the house?" I wondered if he was taking care of himself.

"It's good. Last month Jaxson came over with his friends and put on a new roof for me. Then this morning he was out here shoveling the driveway because we got some snow."

"Jax has been helping you?" I tried to keep the shock out of my voice as I tensed where I sat.

"He comes by every afternoon...ever since my fall."

"What fall?" I leaned forward slightly, gripping the edge of the chair.

"I was trying to put up the Christmas lights and fell off the ladder. I got a bump on the head and a sore bottom, but considering the alternative, I got away easy."

My heart shattered with the thought that my dad could have been seriously hurt, but after a few deep breaths I relaxed knowing he was all right and someone was looking after him. I hadn't called to check on him in months. I never even gave him my new number to call me. He could have died and I wouldn't have known. I thought cutting out my New York life had been best, but now I felt like a horrid daughter. I would have to thank Jax.

We wrapped up the conversation as Andrew arrived and started putting the bags in the cab. I shut everything off in the house and locked it up, then took a deep breath and climbed into the cab.

There was a two-hour delay due to snow in New York, so we sat at the coffee shop and waited as time ticked by slowly. I couldn't shake the bad daughter feeling I was having. I wanted to thank Jax for stepping up, but I was scared of what he would say to me. After all, I snuck out of his house and ran three thousand miles away from him and everyone I knew. I was a coward.

Andrew was waiting in line to get coffee, so I used my time alone to call my voicemail, plugging in Jax's number.

"Thank you for taking care of my dad."

I left the message and hung up my phone, then watched as an elderly couple sitting across from me shared a coffee and muffin. I overheard them saying they were waiting for their kids' flight and I noticed they looked as though they couldn't afford to buy two cups of coffee.

The love they had for each other was clear. The way they looked at each other, it was obvious there was something magical between them. I watched them count their change on the table, confirming what I had first thought, that they didn't have much money. I stood up and cut in front of Andrew in line, as he went to the register. I ordered two blueberry muffins and two coffees. Then I took them to the older couple.

"You nice folks look like you could use a little liquid energy and a snack," I said, placing the coffees in front of them and then the muffins.

"Thank you, dear." The woman nearly had tears in her eyes. "What's your name?"

"My name is Candice. What are your names?" I asked, enthralled with them for some unknown reason.

"I am Helen and this is Henry."

My face fell when I heard the name Henry. It wasn't as common as one would think. The first person who came to mind was Chase, as that was his middle name.

"It's nice to meet you," I said, and started to turn away. Gently, the lady put her hand on mine.

"Excuse me for saying, but you look sad. What's ailing you, dear?" Helen asked, and I didn't know why but I wanted to tell her.

"My fiancé died, and then I turned my back on my best friend. My stomach is full of butterflies and my head is starting to pound as if it is really angry with me about it all right now," I replied in a rush.

"You shouldn't be so hard on yourself. Death affects people differently. Henry is my second husband. My first husband died in Vietnam," she explained. Her husband smiled up at me. "Henry was his sergeant and we fell in love when he came home to take care of me during my loss. Life happens fast. One day I was burying my husband, then three months later I was engaged to Henry. We have been married forty years now. Sometimes you just need to let life happen and not carry around guilt or remorse. Life is too short for that."

She seemed like a wise woman, but who can get married that fast after burying their other half? I couldn't help but feel like I was doing something wrong by not even visiting Chase's grave. I couldn't imagine what it would feel like if I married someone else.

"It was really nice to meet you," I said again, but she pulled my hand to hers once more.

"You know, when I was little there was an old wives' tale that said when you're feeling low or blue, you take a walk in the ocean. It will clean out the mucky feelings you have and let you start anew. Mother used to tell us to stand in the water and make a wish. Maybe you should try it," Helen said, and my heart melted.

I had given up on wishing on the water when I fled from New York. My wishes went unanswered because I still ached from the loss of my other half. Maybe I needed to try again, and I would when I got to New York.

We finally boarded the plane and I slept the whole way. I was exhausted. My body refused to come off its hiatus since I'd learned I would be returning to New York. Andrew admitted he could have taken someone else, but since he enjoyed spending time with me and had become familiar with my background, he had chosen me when they determined the meeting would take place in New York. He told me he felt like I had unfinished business there and needed to deal with it.

We landed at Newark, and decided to rent a car instead of waiting out a six-hour layover. The entire ride seemed long and tedious as I impatiently waited for us to get into the city. When I saw my concrete paradise come into view, we were near the river heading toward the Lincoln Tunnel. A rush of emotion rolled over me, but it wasn't sadness. It shocked me but I felt elated.

"You ready?" Andrew asked, as we drove through the tunnel amidst yellow lights and honking horns.

"Yeah, I think I am."

An hour and three detours from car accidents later, we arrived in front of our hotel. We were staying at the Waldorf Astoria Towers. In all my time in New York I had never been inside the elegant lobby at the Waldorf.

"This room is yours and I am right across the hall from you," Andrew said, handing me my key card in front of the elevator.

"Thanks," I replied, as I took the key and we entered the elevator. As we approached my room, I waved the key card in front of my door. I started to grab the handle of my luggage, but Andrew was already helping me with it. The fact that he was coming into the room with me made me feel a little awkward, but I shrugged it off as a nervous reaction to being back in town. He was always in my house, so I didn't understand why I felt so strange about it here.

"Thanks for bringing that in," I said softly as I walked to the window. I pulled the sheer curtains and looked across the way. The Empire State building was glowing red, white, and blue, as snow fell from the sky.

Andrew stepped up behind me and wrapped his arms around my waist. He rested his chin on my shoulder and I slid my hand over his arms as we stared at the falling snow.

"Thank you," I whispered.

"For what?" Andrew asked softly by my ear.

"For bringing me home. I missed my cement paradise. If you look out at the horizon, there is nothing prettier than my steel and concrete skyline at sunset in the snow."

"It's gorgeous. Anytime I can be of assistance, I would like to help. Get some rest now, and we will hit it hard at seven tomorrow morning in the conference room." He placed a kiss on my cheek before releasing me and taking his bags to his room.

I took in the room. The living room portion had yellow walls with white trim, contrasting nicely with the blue furniture and matching carpet. I had a desk, a dining room table, and even a fireplace. I was in awe already and it was just the living room.

I walked into the bedroom to find the giant king-sized bed, with white sheets and comforter, along with the blue and white on the walls and the blue carpet. I was starting to think about painting my home in California the same color. The toilet sat in the middle of the bathroom and there was a tub to the right and a glass shower to the left. There was even a remote controlled radio for my long relaxing baths.

I found a list on the bed of services and amenities, then called immediately and scheduled a spa appointment. Andrew had said whatever I wanted was on the company's dime. I wanted a massage bad enough to let them pay for it. After I hung up, I noticed the living room was bigger than my entire house in California and I suddenly felt overwhelmed.

I grabbed my suitcase and changed into a pair of skinny jeans, my black calf-high Uggs, and a gray and white geometric sweater. I fixed my make-up, then grabbed my A-line black coat to go outside and get some New York air. Once I was ready to go, I thought about asking Andrew to come since I was familiar with the area and he wasn't, but I needed to clear my head. The words Helen had said made me think that maybe I was a sitting duck: I was only floating on the water because no one had come to be my life raft.

Those words even had me thinking about how Helen's story would make a great book. I could write her story, but that was part of my life with Chase. Anyway, anti-virus sales were my life now.

I set out on Lexington Avenue, deciding to walk a few blocks and soak up the city I loved. I could still smell the hot dog vendor's cart that sat on the corner during the day. I could imagine the horns honking as cabs waited in traffic that never moved. I stuck out my arms and spun myself as the snow began to fall.

I smiled when I came to a stop sign, then continued walking. I saw the Bull & Bear when I rounded the corner and decided a drink would be wonderful. I walked inside and took off my coat before sitting at the bar.

"Black Russian, please," I called to the bartender.

"Do I know you?" A strange man spoke with a slurred voice.

"No, I don't think you do," I replied sweetly, as the bartender brought me my drink.

"Yes, I do. You were Chase Matson's fiancé." He stumbled over his words. "I am so sorry for your loss. He was a great man." Chills rolled down my spine. I downed my drink and ordered another.

"Sir, I just want to enjoy a drink and not talk about anything with anyone," I whispered, and he nodded. He slowly got up and whipped out his cell phone as I downed another drink of numbing juice. I looked over and saw him on the phone with someone, a new drink in his hand.

I tried to place him as I ordered another shot. I stared at his demeanor and knew he had been on the force, but I couldn't recall him. Maybe because I'd already had three drinks by then and was feeling no pain. The room had moments of fuzziness, but I wasn't drunk, merely tipsy. I ordered another and the bartender advised me to eat or slow down. I was reluctant, but ordered a burger, since he seemed serious about cutting me off if I kept going.

The burger and fries were delicious. They didn't have food like this in California. I promised myself that I would eat at every place I had been missing before I went home. My phone lit up and I saw a message from an unknown number and instantly felt a twinge of guilt. It had to be Jax. I just knew it had to be him because I had called him. I wasn't going to check the message, so I cleared it and placed my phone back down.

The drunk man returned to his seat near me and smiled every few minutes, but had left me alone. I was grateful. I couldn't take any more people telling me how sorry they were, or how great of a guy Chase was. I know they felt it was polite, but I had heard it enough.

I ordered another drink as my phone lit up again. The same thing as before, just a message and nothing else. Maybe he was finally telling me off. My voicemail only holds sixty second messages. I downed my drink and ordered another when I heard a voice behind me.

"She is done drinking. Get her a coffee and water, please."

It took a few minutes for my alcohol-riddled brain to realize I was not going to get my drink. I spun on my stool and came face to face with a detective, his badge hanging around his neck.

"Why are you...cut me off?" I slurred. The room spun.

"Ms. Carson, I think we should get some water into you." The young, black haired, blue-eyed detective cloned himself in my vision.

"You don't drunk me." I spoke with my finger aimed at one of him.

"Ms. Carson, I am Detective Mark Stone. You may not remember me. I worked with Chase on a few cases before he passed away."

"I know you, but I don't want to talk about Chase," I slurred.

"I am not here to talk about him, but I am here to help you sober up and get you home."

"Did the drunk guy call you?" I pointed at an empty bar stool. *When did that guy leave?* My brain was foggy and I couldn't make sense of anything.

"Something like that. May I join you?" Mark asked, as I spun and nearly fell off my stool. We then talked for about two hours while the fog cleared from my head. He seemed like a good guy. He didn't bring up Chase again or try to get in my pants, so he was *A-plus* in my book.

I was as sober as I was going to get, and my words were coming together better as exhaustion tore through me. Jetlag and alcohol are not a good mix when you have a meeting at seven in the morning.

"I need to get going. Thank you for the water and conversation," I muttered, as I tried to put my coat on. I watched as he texted someone on his phone, then he stood and helped me into my coat.

"Can I walk you somewhere, or get you a cab?" Mark asked.

"You're sweet, but I can manage," I replied.

"Ms. Carson, if you need anything while you are here, please don't hesitate to call." He handed me his card. I took it and smiled at him. I didn't know if he was just being nice, or if this was part of the code; the brothers in blue take care of the wives and families of a dead officer. I didn't want to know, because I didn't want to think about it.

I stepped out to see there was snow and rain falling from the sky. For one fleeting moment, I was home. I looked up at the night sky as the rain and snow mix fell onto my forehead and cheeks. I closed my eyes and made a wish on the water, that I would have the courage and strength to love, and recognize love, when and if I ever found it again. I didn't want to wind up alone pining for a man who was in Heaven.

When I opened my eyes again, I started toward the hotel. I must have missed the curb as I slipped and fell. Mark was behind me in a moment, helping me stand back up.

"Thank you," I whispered, turning crimson from embarrassment.

"Don't thank me yet. I was merely doing a favor for someone." Mark nodded above my head.

"What are you talking about?" I asked, wondering just how drunk I still was.

"Hello, Candy," a familiar voice called from behind me. Shivers went down my spine. My stomach clenched and my body betrayed me as his voice reverberated through me. I turned around and faced the music of the song I had chosen to write.

"Hello, Jaxson."

Chapter Ten

My voice was barely a whisper as I spoke his name. He looked delectable in a pair of jeans and his black and red tri-climate jacket. He was showing a five o'clock shadow, but there was nothing else different about him. I looked into his eyes, the same ones that could tear a secret from my soul.

He didn't look pissed, but that could be because my belly was warm and fuzzy with the remnants of the alcohol I had downed in the bar. Then I remembered there was still a man behind me. I turned and glared at Mark.

"Your job is done now," I whispered angrily.

"Sorry, but it's part of the code between men," Mark stated, as he shook hands with Jax and then walked off.

The awkwardness had descended, blanketing me with a thick layer of not knowing what to say or think. I wondered if he would follow if I ran.

"I am going back to my hotel now," I said a little too loudly. "Thanks for sending the babysitter."

The reflection in the windows of buildings and cars told me Jax was following me. I turned the corner and walked into the hotel. He followed me there, too. I climbed into the elevator and he stood across from me, looking like a dream while we rose up from floor to floor.

As I exited the elevator and arrived at my door, I took out my key card and waved it. The lock wouldn't work. I tried waving it again, but nothing happened. Jax took it from my hand and slowly waved it over the door across the way and it opened.

I suddenly felt like a moron; I was trying to get into Andrew's room. Jax opened the door and I walked inside. I took off my coat and dumped it on the nearest chair, then went to the phone. I ordered a bottle of vodka and a variety platter with fruits and veggies.

"Do you really think you need more alcohol?" Jax asked from the blue couch he had made himself at home on.

"If you are going to be here, then yes," I replied and smirked.

Why was I so angry with him?

Every emotion I had seemed to amplify a thousand times whenever Jax was near.

"If I leave, how do I know you won't drink yourself into oblivion?"

"I have a daddy, I don't need another." I rolled my eyes.

Jax stood up and walked over to me. He wrapped his arms around me and I fought to get free. The warmth he carried overpowered me and I melted into him. I was torn between wanting to sigh in relief and cry in frustration. When he let me go, I walked over to the window.

"How did you find me?" I whispered.

"Your dad told me you were coming. Did you think I wouldn't come and find you?" Jax asked, and I closed my eyes. He walked up behind me and whispered into my ear. "Candice, a few months ago I came out to California to bring you home, but you seemed so happy without me in your new life. I left you alone so you could be happy there."

Guilt invaded my core. I had no right to be angry or bitter with him, but I was. I had no reason to feel ashamed for my actions because I was just trying to survive, but I felt like I was the gum on the bottom of his shoes. My guilt festered into anger as his warmth invaded me and I realized how much I had truly lost.

"Don't you have a girlfriend you should be tucking into bed? Isn't it past her bedtime?"

I immediately wanted to call back my words. My alcohol infused brain didn't put a filter on my lips. Now he would know I had been stalking him online, and I didn't want him to know. I didn't even want to see him.

"She knows where I am," Jax replied.

"Does she know you've had your penis in me? Some girls get mad about that kind of thing," I retorted.

He didn't reply; he merely went back and sat on the couch. He picked up his phone and called someone.

"Hey, babe," Jax said into the phone. "I know it's late, but wanted you to know I am going to stay with Candice tonight."

I stared at him. I never asked him to stay and I was not going to let him. There was no way any woman in her right mind would let a catch as great at Jax stay with me overnight.

"She has had a little too much to drink, and we need to talk."

I was strangely affected when I saw Jax smile. Whatever she'd said had made him happy, and I couldn't fathom why until he spoke again.

"Okay, Vanessa. I love you, too. I will see you tomorrow." He hung up, and I flipped out.

"Get out!" I screamed. Rage was filling my veins and I felt sick to my stomach. I ran to the bathroom and crumpled to the floor in front of the toilet. It wasn't a minute later that Jax was standing in the doorway. "You have to leave. I need you gone," I pleaded.

"Tell me why," Jax replied, crossing his arms.

"You just have to go. Go home to her."

"Candy—"

"I hate you, Jax," I screamed, sobbing, and he walked inside the bathroom. He picked me up off the floor and carried me into the bedroom. He held me tightly to him as I cried harder than I had cried in months. It was a relief to get it out, but the new pain that followed was gut wrenching. I had lost my friendship with Jax, and allowed him to think he was better off without me. *Were we better off without each other?*

He placed me on the bed and grabbed the trash can and set it in front of me in case I puked. I watched as he pulled the chair from the desk and sat before me. I had seen both Jax and Chase do this with interrogations. I didn't know if I was ready to answer the question he surely had for me.

"Why?" he asked, and my emotional well was filling up again. If he didn't leave I was going to shoot off like a rocket. I could not control my words and actions anymore. I was seriously regretting the decision I made to go get drinks.

"Jax, please go. I can't be around you."

"Candy, I am not leaving until you tell me why you hate me. What did I do? Is this because I have someone?" Jax asked, and I hit my breaking point.

"I hate you because you love her. I hate you because you are happy. I hate you because it's not fair that everyone has moved on. But if I do, it disrespects Chase. I hate you because you were my friend and Chase's partner and you are still here while he is gone. But most of all, I hate you because I love you."

I ran into the bathroom crying so hard that I was dry heaving. I didn't mean to tell him all that. I didn't even know it had been boiling up until the words left my lips. As I calmed my cries, I listened and heard the door shut. I closed my eyes, thankful he'd left, but I felt alone and depressed instantly.

I cleaned myself up and took a shower. I don't know why Jax pulls such strong emotions from me, but he does. What I feel with Andrew as my friend is nothing compared to what I feel for Jax. Maybe it is longevity. Maybe, one day in twenty years, I will feel that way with Andrew.

I took the robe off the back of the door and put it on as I exited the bathroom, feeling like I had been hit by an emotional truck. When I stepped around the corner, Jax was still in the chair. He was staring at the bed and didn't look up at me.

"Please leave," I begged.

He looked over at me with an emotionless mask on his face. I snagged a water off the tray of alcohol and snacks that had been delivered, and climbed into the bed. I pulled the comforter over me and stacked the pillows to get comfortable. I tried to wait him out. I tried to make a point, but the jetlag and alcohol won, so I drifted off to sleep.

I woke up a few hours later, and saw the clock said six fifty-two. I was late. I jumped out of bed, feeling my hangover behind my eyes. I ran for the shower. I took the quickest, coldest shower of my life, then put on a sweater dress and my fuzzy knee-high boots. It wasn't the greatest outfit, but it would do.

I heard a knock on the door and yelled, "Two minutes," to Andrew, who I assumed was knocking. I threw on make-up and grabbed my notes, then ran for the door to be greeted by Andrew, who looked well-rested.

"You ready?" he asked, looking like a million bucks. He handed me coffee, as he did almost every morning, and I struggled to put everything in my bag.

"I'm ready. Go on down. I will be right behind you. They were supposed to set up conference room A, and the slide show and presentation packets should already be there. I just need a second to pull myself together," I muttered in a rush.

"You will be great," Andrew said, wrapping an arm around me, pulling me in for a hug and placing a kiss on my cheek. "See you down there." He gave me a wink and walked down toward the elevator.

I turned back around and headed for my suitcase in the closet. I pulled out my Tylenol, and took two. Then I grabbed a bottle of water from the tray and chugged it. When I walked around the corner to the living room to get my coat, I found Jax standing in the doorway.

"I thought you left," I whispered.

"I thought we should talk while you were sober." A look of exhaustion crossed his face. I saw his Saint Michael necklace and instantly flashed back to the blonde he had waiting at home.

"Jax—"

"Who was that man at the door?"

"Andrew," I whispered, as if I was being scolded. I did not explain who Andrew was to me and honestly I didn't know what I would say if he asked me. I couldn't tell Jax that he was my new best friend.

"Candice—"

I put my hand up to stop him. "I have to go to the conference downstairs. I am already late. Whatever you have to say can—and will—wait!"

Then I headed out the door, leaving him behind as he continued to call my name.

The first day at the conference left my head swimming. They wanted answers to questions I hadn't even thought of.

I will have to take the time to study up tonight and be ready for tomorrow.

"You ready for dinner?" Andrew asked, and I nodded my agreement as I finished writing the last of my notes.

"I will meet you in the lobby in one hour," I said as we parted ways. Andrew had to finish cleaning up and I needed a hot shower.

I went upstairs and into my room. I caught myself looking for Jax, which was dumb on my part. I had told him to leave, that I hated him. I even told him I was in love with him. I was a walking contradiction.

I got ready to go to dinner by picking out a black, one shoulder, chiffon A-line dress that matched my coat and a pair of Tabitha Simmons Bailey heels. I had seen them in the movie *Just Go With It*, and had to have them. They cost me more money than I paid for my last car, but they were my one vice, and I thought they were worth every penny. I had waited for a night out to wear them and I had it, here and now.

I headed downstairs and met Andrew in the lobby. He grinned at me and it made me smile, too. He took my hand and twirled me in the lobby as he took in my dress.

"It should be a crime to be this beautiful." He spoke with a silvery tone, as a smirk traveled across his face.

"Could you be any cheesier?" I asked with a laugh.

"Let me try. Did it hurt?"

"Did what hurt?"

"Did it hurt when you fell from Heaven?"

"I admit it. You can be cheesier!"

Andrew placed a kiss on my knuckles when he drew my hand up to his lips. Then he released it to help me into my coat.

"I must be the luckiest boss in the world since I have you in my office and in my arms," Andrew said, wrapping his arms around me.

I was as uneasy as I was flattered. I turned and nodded my head, telling him, "Let's go," and he quickly took the lead.

The View was a restaurant that sat atop the Marriott Marquis in Times Square. Upon arrival, I saw Detective Mark Stone talking to a woman with black hair and blue eyes. She seemed to be upset about something. I tried to look away, but the way he looked at her spoke volumes of the love he had for her. I suddenly felt alone and empty. No one would look at me like that again if I didn't pull my head out of my butt.

"Ms. Carson," Mark called out, so Andrew and I walked toward him.

"Detective Stone," I said politely. I had a million other things I *could* have called him, but thought I would be nice and refer to his actual title.

"Ms. Carson, have you met our lovely Assistant District Attorney, Brooklyn Montgomery?"

I was shocked when Brooklyn smiled at me. She was young and looked like the girls I had seen on the news. She had a gorgeous flawless face with long black hair and bright blue eyes.

"No, I haven't had the pleasure. I'm Candice Carson." I held out my hand for her. "This is my boss, Andrew Thomas." Andrew stuck his hand out to greet them both.

"Candice-Leigh Carson?" Brooklyn asked.

"Yes, ma'am, that is me," I replied with a smile.

"I am so sorry for your loss. Chase was a great detective and a wonderful man."

I wanted to roll my eyes. I had grown to hate words of comfort when it related to someone who'd died. I would always be professional, but I had to wonder if people would ever stop bringing it up. Every time someone mentioned his job I felt a twinge of pain and imagined the baby who might look like him.

"We are headed up to have dinner. Would you like to join us?" Andrew asked, as I took his arm.

Both Brooklyn and Mark agreed, and we headed upstairs in the elevator. Thankfully, the restaurant was able to upgrade us to a larger table. Andrew and I sat on one side while Mark and Brooklyn sat on the other.

Dinner was delicious and time flew as we engaged in conversation about the differences between California and New York. I looked at my watch and it was nearly ten. I needed to get back and get the information packets done for the next day. I was getting ready to excuse myself and head back when Mark spoke up.

"Candice, would you join me in bringing back a nightcap for everyone from the bar since our waiter is busy?"

I nodded and excused myself from the table. He walked around and held out his elbow for me to take as we headed toward the bar.

Once we reached the bar, Mark kept walking until we were in a darkened corner where we couldn't be seen from the lobby. We were essentially hidden from Andrew and Brooklyn.

"What did you do to my partner?" Mark asked.

"Who is your partner?"

"Jax is helping me with a couple cases. I need him clearheaded and on the right track. A simple night with you and he is ready to blow an investigation and murder someone. He has spent months getting in this far."

"Who does he want to kill?" I whispered, as if someone might have heard.

"One of the cases I am working on involved his old partner. I can't talk about it right now, but he is balls deep in it. Whatever you did to him last night, *undo* it so he keeps a clear head and doesn't get killed."

I nodded that I understood, even though I didn't have a clue what he was talking about. The words echoed in my head that Jax could be killed. I asked Mark to convey my apologies and I left.

Half an hour in a cab and I was sitting in front of Jax's house. The word's *officer slain* had been captioned on newspapers when Chase died. I could still see them in my head, only this time I envisioned Jax's face on the cover and I wanted to throw up.

I couldn't breathe, thinking something might happen to Jax. I felt dizzy when I thought about what Mark said. My heart ached. I had been such a bitch to him, when none of it was his fault.

I climbed out of the cab and the driver sped off as I approached the door. I rang the doorbell, but no one answered. I located the tiny plastic frog that was in his potted plant at the door and found the spare key below it. I opened the door and let myself in.

I turned on the lights and looked around the house. Not much had changed. There were still pictures of me and Chase on the mantle with Jax. There was a new picture with Jax and my dad that sat beside the one of me blowing a kiss at him. There was also a centerpiece picture of him and the blonde.

I went upstairs and stared at the room I had snuck out of. I sat down on the bed and began to wonder what would have happened between us if I had stayed. Would Jax have filled my heart and made me a better person like Helen at the airport had said, or would I have ended our friendship like I had when I ran?

I saw my luggage that I'd left behind, sitting inside the edge of the closet. I had expected him to toss everything, but he didn't. I walked into his bedroom and saw a picture of the blonde sitting beside his bed. I turned back to see two toothbrushes in the bathroom and my heart sank.

My head started spinning with phrases like *Jax might die,* and *he doesn't want you anymore.* I walked back downstairs and sat on the couch. I was getting ready to call a cab when I heard a noise outside. I froze, wondering who it was. Then there was a key in the door and my heart started racing. I watched as the doorknob opened so slowly. My palms had grown sweaty and my heart raced. My stomach tightened with each thought of seeing Jax.

Then the door opened and in walked a beautiful, long-legged blonde, who was kissing Jax. He had his arms around her waist and was pulling her into the house backward as she jumped to wrap her legs around him. I was about to vomit.

Chapter Eleven

"Candice?" Jax asked, when he pulled his face off the blonde long enough to see me on the couch. I was so overwhelmed with emotion. The words that he was going to die were floating in my head, making me panic as I took in the woman on his arm with jealousy. My eyes burned as they filled with tears, but I couldn't say a word. I merely held my arms clutched to my body.

"Candice, what are you doing here?" Jax asked, but I couldn't say a word. "Vanessa, take my truck and head home. I think Candice and I need to talk." She protested and pouted her lips. I should have left and walked away, but the words echoed in my head that Jax would die and I would never be able to tell him what he meant to me.

He finally convinced Vanessa to leave. I inhaled deeply and knew it was time to say something. I had to let go and just let life carry me. I closed my eyes and tried to calm myself, but it wasn't working. When I opened my eyes, Jax was sitting on the coffee table in front of me. He looked worried, which was a relief, considering I was being a cock-block or whatever they call those people.

"Candice, are you all right?" Jax asked in a whisper, placing his hand on my knee. Fire strummed through me, and I lost control of my thoughts.

"You can't die!" I demanded and his hand left my knee.

"What are you talking about?" Jax asked, as he stood up and turned on the fireplace. I rose and threw my clutch on the couch. I pulled off my coat and dropped it as well. Jax turned and looked me up and down. It was like breathing fresh air to see him look at me the way he used to.

"You know exactly what I am talking about. Mark talked to me at dinner tonight."

Jax walked around the coffee table, took my hand and led me upstairs, into the spare bedroom where we had made love. I watched as he opened the closet and pulled out my luggage.

"Thank you for staying at Chez Monroe. Let us call you a cab," Jax murmured, and handed me my bags. I deserved this for what I had done. I deserved a lot worse actually.

"Jaxson—"

"Candice," he began angrily, "I don't know what you are doing here, but let me tell you what I have done. I buried my best friend, then I found comfort in the arms of his girl, my other best friend. I thought it was the start of something that would lead to a happy ending. Then you snuck out of the house, moved three thousand miles away, and cut me out of your life. Then you show up here, get plastered and tell me you hate me because you love me. I moved on the best way I knew how and you should, too. It's not healthy to hold onto Chase this way."

A single tear fell from my eye and I had no control over myself anymore. I walked right up to Jax and ripped opened his blue button down shirt to take in the St. Michaels necklace he was still wearing. I took the necklace in my hand like I'd seen in the photo and pulled, but Jax didn't come down to me.

"Do you love her?" I whispered as I held the pendant in my hand.

"Does it matter?" Jax replied, as he pulled my hand off his necklace.

"Jax, please," I begged with tears in my eyes.

"You are not listening to me. It is not healthy for you to look me up online and come to my house whenever you want. I loved you, Candice. I loved everything about you. Chase dying made me see that you were the reason why I never settled down. Then I saw the real you, the one who runs like a coward and hides when things get real."

"Jax, please!"

"I don't want anyone like that in my life. I deserve to be happy, not to be hurt. Candice, you left months ago, and left a lot of broken hearts on your way out of town. I understood the anger from Christina, but to flee because of that and not turn to your friends and family was wrong. You stayed away too long, so we moved on, Candice, and we are getting by just fine without you. Maybe you should go back to California."

I was speechless. I'd had my heart broken many times, but never by Jax. He must really love her.

"Is this a see-ya-later?" I asked, hoping for a positive answer, even though I doubted it. I missed Jax in my life; he was my rock of strength and my sounding board when I needed to vent. He was my best friend. The ache in my chest said that I loved him as I loved Chase, but how could that be possible? How can someone love two people the same way?

"Candice, this is not a see-ya-later. This is where you say goodbye, you go home, and you let us get on with our lives. You bailed on us the first time you flew out of New York. It is time for history to repeat itself."

I grabbed my bags and carried them down the stairs while Jax called me a cab to come pick me up. I should have expected this. I had done everything he said and then I invaded his house and his life. I should just accept this and go on, but I couldn't.

"Jax, I am really sorry for any pain I caused you."

He merely looked at me and nodded his head as he wandered into the kitchen and grabbed the coffee grounds. I smiled as I saw the Tim Hortons' bag he pulled out and remembered a time when we would have been enjoying that together, our veins pumping the caffeinated goodness while we shared smiles, laughs, and secrets.

"Jax, thank you for taking care of my dad. If you will send me the bill for the roof, I would like to pay for it."

"No!" Jax answered sharply. "He was a second father to me growing up. I owe him more than a roof. You can pay for the next one."

"Are you always going to hate me?" I whispered, as there was so much hostility in his voice. Jax hung his head and stopped what he was doing. He took a deep breath and then looked my way.

"Candice, I don't know what you want me to say. If I say yes, then that will hurt you and if I say no, you will still be hurt, wondering what you might do to make me not hate you. If I say nothing, then your writer brain will concoct all kinds of other words for hate and try them all. You should just go home and let it go."

The cab pulled up as thunder roared. The temperature wasn't low enough yet for more snow to fall. I was finally going to get my raindrops. I took my bags and handed them to the cab driver who took them out and placed them in the trunk. I put on my coat and grabbed my clutch. I went to the front door and Jax followed with his fresh cup of coffee.

I got down the steps when the sky opened up. I closed my eyes to the invigorating feeling of rain cascading down my face. I decided to make a wish on the water: to keep Jax safe from harm. I didn't make a wish for me this time, as his needs were greater than mine.

I knew standing out in the rain I must have looked like a fool, but I needed him to stay safe. I needed the peace of mind to know that even though I threw away a twenty-year friendship, he would be happy while he grew old and gray.

"What are you wishing for now?" Jax called out behind me, as the cab waited to leave.

"I wished you a long, happy, and healthy life," I yelled, as the sky roared. "Despite what you may think, I do love you. It just took a long time to figure it out." I went to the cab. As I got to the door, I threw my clutch inside. Drenched to the bone, I ran back up to the porch and wrapped my wet arms around Jax's neck and hugged him to me. He wrapped his one free arm around me and hugged me back.

As I pulled back, I placed my lips on his. He resisted at first, but then kissed me back with one hand in my hair. That same spark of electricity came to life and my skin ran hot. When we pulled away, we were breathless, but full of goodbye.

"I needed the good to go with the bad," I muttered, and ran for the cab.

When I got to the hotel, Andrew was in the lobby pacing with the concierge. He looked frazzled and Mark was with both of them, seemingly annoyed.

"Where the hell have you been?" Andrew shouted above the people mingling as I walked over to them. I handed my luggage to the concierge and he sent the luggage upstairs.

"What is the problem?" I was mortified by his shouting as people stared at us. He looked furious; it was an expression I had never seen on him before.

"You bailed on us at dinner and then you didn't answer your phone. You need to always answer your phone when I call. What is wrong with you? Where have you been? Why didn't you tell us where you were going?" Andrew glared at me.

"What the hell is with everyone today?" I retorted and went toward the elevator. I was so angry with him that I didn't even notice Mark climbing in the elevator with me. I stared at the walls as my back faced the doors. I put my hands on my hips and tried to take slow, deep breaths.

I didn't know what was with the game of twenty questions when I entered the hotel, but I knew I was not going to stand there and be yelled at like some child. The worst part was I didn't know if my friend Andrew was angry or if this was my boss Andrew who was angry. Either way, I refused to hear it tonight.

I exited on my floor and walked quickly to my room. I walked in so fast I didn't notice that Mark had caught the door with his shoe. I grabbed my luggage from the entrance and dragged it to the bedroom while Mark made himself at home in the living room.

"Why are you here?" I shouted from the bedroom, and a few moments later Mark walked in the doorway.

"You and I both know why I am here." He responded in a low tone.

"If you are looking to get laid, I am not your girl," I snapped, pushing the luggage into the closet.

"I think Brooklyn might murder me if I did, and since she is a prosecutor, she would know how to get away with it," Mark replied with a smile.

I couldn't return his smile as everything inside me was held together by fractured tape.

"Why are you here?" I asked again, as my voice quivered.

"I am here because you need me to be here." Mark walked over to me, enveloping me in his arms and I immediately broke.

"He's gone," I murmured through my tears.

"Sweetheart, Chase has been gone for months."

"Jax is gone. He hates me, and I deserve it." I cried into Mark and even started the dry heaving again.

Mark led me into the living room. He sat me on the couch as a loud banging told us someone was at the door. Mark went to answer the door and I could hear Andrew, but his voice was muffled. When Mark came back, he was alone and I was grateful.

"Tell me what happened," Mark stated, as I calmed myself.

"I went to him, with an open heart and open arms. He had the blonde, Vanessa, with him, but he sent her home when he saw me. I thought that was a good thing, until he said it was over. He said goodbye. I thought I had broken what we had and ran because of it, but the truth is I hadn't broken us, not until I ran. Now he loves her and I love him." I started crying again and Mark got me a glass of water.

"I'm sorry, sweetheart. I didn't know you felt that way for him," Mark muttered, as he pulled me into his arms on the couch. He rubbed my back and just let me cry. It was the nicest thing a stranger had done in a long time.

"This is worse than when Chase died. I know Chase is in a better place and is happy in the sky. He is probably running practical jokes on the other angels. I think Chase wanted me to be with Jax. It was in his letter, but I was too scared that I would lose Jax as well. Chase left me and I was devastated. I couldn't let Jax leave me, and hurt me that way, so I left him. Now he is gone, but I will always wonder if Jax is happy, whereas I know Chase is."

Mark curled me into his chest and clutched me with one arm as he used his phone with another. Duty called; it always did, but Mark made no move to leave.

"Candice, maybe he is not the one for you," Mark said as he stroked my back.

"No. He is my other half. He was always the one for me. When we were together, we were the three legs of a tripod. We fit together to make a whole. Now, there are two of us left and we could form an arch, or something, but we are broken and the pieces no longer fit."

I cried into Mark for the next hour or so. I had to give him credit; other than messing with his phone every now and then, I had his undivided attention and relished the feeling of being comforted.

I had made lots of wishes on the water as I aged, but I never really prayed. I prayed and asked Chase to let go of my heart and allow me to move on. I don't know why I felt like he had my heart, but I wasn't whole. Until I was, I couldn't put him or Jax behind me.

Mark pulled me tighter into him and pulled the blanket down that was on top of the couch. He covered me up and rubbed my back until I fell fast asleep.

Chapter Twelve

I woke up to the smell of coffee in the air. I sat up and realized that I was late for the conference. I was going to get fired on this trip. I rubbed my eyes and looked around but didn't see anyone. I shrugged off the blanket and went into the bedroom where I ran into Mark.

"I smell coffee," I whispered, not really knowing what to say.

"I had some sent up. I sent Andrew with whatever papers he found to the conference. You and I are going to take a day off," Mark said with a smile.

"All right, but I am supposed to meet my dad," I whispered. It was my birthday after all, even if I didn't feel much like celebrating. Mark nodded his head and I walked past him to the bathroom and climbed in the shower.

An hour later, I had showered, straightened my brown and blonde hair, and put on make-up. I was dressed in a white long-sleeve shirt with a black leather vest over it. I had my skinny jeans on and my knee high leather biker boots. They said we might get more snow if the temperature continued to drop, so I was prepared for anything. I grabbed my black jacket and headed into the living room.

"You look like a million bucks," Mark stated, and I gave him a shrug.

"I feel like scum."

"Let's see if we can't turn that frown upside down." He handed me fresh coffee in a Tim Hortons' cup. I almost jumped for joy with the first sip. I missed the morning ritual of going to Tim Hortons with the guys.

I inhaled the aroma as Mark took my hand. He already had my purse as he ushered me out the door.

"Are we in a hurry?" I asked, as we sped toward the elevator.

"Well, I have an itinerary. We have deadlines." Mark laughed and slowed down.

"I am all too familiar with deadlines," I retorted, as the elevator descended. I didn't really know what to say. The last year of my life had been a roller coaster of events and emotions, but I finally found where I belonged and who I belonged with. That is the funny thing about life. It never asks what you want. It holds up a cookie and if you don't grab it in time, you don't get the whole cookie. In some cases you don't even get a crumb.

As we exited the elevator, I saw my dad. He was very skinny with salt and pepper hair. When I left he had about fifty pounds of excess weight on him. I was elated to see him, but very worried about him as well. My emotions overflowed, and I ran to him.

My dad wasn't there for me very much after my mom died. I didn't blame him for it, and always wanted a better relationship with him. Maybe this was the new path in life I was supposed to take.

"Candy Cane," my dad whispered, enveloping me in his arms.

"Daddy, it is so good to see you," I murmured in his ear, before placing a kiss on his cheek.

"Candy, you look tired," he said, and I turned to introduce him to Mark. After they shook hands, I hugged my dad again. I was so glad to see him. I hadn't even realized how much I missed him until then.

"Where are we going, guys?" I asked, standing between the two.

"You two are headed to The Cafeteria to eat while I take care of something. I will meet you there in an hour," Mark said, glancing at his phone.

My dad and I grabbed a cab and headed for The Cafeteria. It was my birthday, and I wanted banana split waffles.

"Dad, have you been eating enough?" I asked as the cab drove through the congested city.

"It's the new medicine the doctor gave me. It is supposed to help control my overactive thyroid, but hasn't stopped the weight loss. Since you brought up how I look, I want to know why my daughter looks the same right now as she did when her mother and Chase died."

"Jax," I replied in a whisper.

"Want me to kick his ass?" my dad asked, acting as serious as he could while I laughed, trying to imagine my sixty-year-old father with his toothpick arms trying to fight my toned and tanned police detective.

"No, Dad, I did this. It's my fault. I was thinking about it this morning, though. I may see if I can go back to the publishing company and write more books. I don't think the new job is going to work. I tried to make it fit me, instead of letting the job mold to me. I can't avoid it. I can't run from it any longer. I am a writer."

"Really, Candy? Does that mean you will move back here?" My dad actually looked hopeful. I stared into his brown eyes and warmth ran over me with the love and hope he saw in me.

"I actually thought you could come to California to live with me."

I was met with silence. He acted as though I had not said a word about his moving. I guess I always knew he would never leave New York, but I wanted to take care of him. I was finally old enough, and had suffered enough loss to know why raising me was hard for him. I wanted to help him, but maybe I could hire someone to look in on him from time to time.

As we exited the cab and walked inside The Cafeteria, I saw Michelle. She was waiting at the door. She wrapped me in her arms and nearly knocked the breath out of me with her excitement.

"I got your message, Candy. You will always be my daughter. No matter what your reasons are, it is your life...but I'm so glad you are home."

I wrapped my arms around her and hugged the only real mom I ever had. My mom had passed away when I was seven, and Jax's parents died a few years later. Michelle was everyone's mom.

I pulled back to see Christina standing by a table with a carrier. My face must have fallen because Michelle wrapped her arm around me and whispered in my ear.

"She is not staying for breakfast with us, but we thought you might want to meet Chelle Matson."

"No, I really don't," I muttered under my breath, as I was escorted by Michelle and my dad to the table. Christina immediately busied herself with getting the baby out of the car seat.

The breath was knocked out of me when Christina held up her baby. Chelle had blonde hair like Chase, blue eyes, and his smile. I wanted to cry when I saw him in her. She was a chunky baby with an aura of happiness around her.

"Do you want to hold her?" Christina asked, and I glared at her. I didn't really know how to feel about her, or this, and was trying to let life lead me instead of me being in control.

I looked at Michelle and my dad who seemed so happy to see the baby. I bit the bullet as Christina put the baby in my arms. I stared down at her while they started putting two tables together in front of the glass bay doors. As baby Chelle pulled my hair and laughed, I couldn't help but see her dad's mischievous side in her already.

"You look good with a baby," Mark said as he walked by.

"I take it you took care of whatever it was and now I get a day of fun, right?" I asked with a wink. My heartbreak had been lifted with the weight of a baby in my arms. Chase may have died, but I could see him inside her.

She was going to be a handful, and heaven help the boys who came near her, because the whole NYPD would be supervising their dates.

"I did what I needed to do. Brooklyn is coming to join us. I hope that is okay," Mark said. I nodded as I looked back down at baby Chelle. I cooed and bounced her as if she was my own when I felt a warmth rumble through my veins. My face faltered and my pulse hitched. I didn't know where this was coming from. I turned and looked around, but saw nothing out of place.

I looked out the window and I swore Chase was standing on the corner looking at us. I closed my eyes, and shook my head. When I opened my eyes, he was gone. I took it as a sign that he was happy we were all together, even if I secretly wanted to pluck every red hair out of Christina's head and feed her nothing but Krispy Kremes for a month. That would fix the after-baby hourglass body that was unfair to women everywhere.

The thought of fattening Christina up put a smile on my face and baby Chelle laughed with me, as if she knew what I was thinking. Brooklyn came in and looked at baby Chelle over my shoulder and gave Mark *the look*. The one where she explains her clock is ticking without saying a word.

As the seats filled up, I sat down with Chelle. She became instantly fussy and I stood back up. I surrendered to her tiny ineffectual whimpers and cuddled her while we bounced. I watched Andrew come in with a smile for me and the baby. I could tell he was in a better mood than he had been the night before.

I felt him before I knew he was there. I could feel Jax's energy and confidence, his comfort and smell, his essence that made my mouth water. I could imagine his heart pounding as my body thrummed to the beat. I turned and looked ahead at the entrance and there he was.

He stood before me with a semi-smile. He was wearing a white button-down with the sleeves rolled up. His tanned skin screamed at me to taste it. His gray eyes bore into me as he walked toward me. I had to look down at baby Chelle and force myself to breathe.

"I told you she loved him. Now pay up," I heard Brooklyn say to Christina.

"Losing your breath is not love. It's a lack of oxygen," Christina replied.

I tuned them all out and focused on the baby. She was a wiggly little thing. I felt Jax's breath on my shoulder as he leaned over to look at baby Chelle. She cooed and giggled at him. The familiarity was evident I knew he had been around this baby.

"Hey, little bit," Jax said, as he pretended to eat her hand and she giggled. Her laughter was infectious and soon we were all laughing, too. Jax took her from my arms and handed her back to Christina.

"We need a minute," Jax said before he took my hand, leading me outside. We weren't really away from anyone, as they could see through the bay doors and my friends and family could hear us. The glass did not keep noise out.

"We should talk about last night," Jax started, and I put my finger on his lips.

"It's fine, Jax. I will be fine. It's over and done with. Let's just eat and get on with our lives." I started to walk away, but Jax grabbed my arm and pulled me back and I fell into his chest as he planted his lips over mine.

A rush of electricity flooded me. I tangled my fingers in Jax's brown hair and pulled him where I wanted him as his velvet tongue coaxed me to open up for him. I allowed the coffee he'd been drinking to invade my senses. My clit pulsed with my heart and I could barely breathe. I felt every hard inch of him as he pulled me tightly to him.

"I am so pissed at you," he muttered breathlessly.

"Are you so pissed that you want to spank me? Anger can be kinky," I whispered as I heard the *awww* from our family and friends who had been watching behind the glass doors.

Jax merely smiled at the comment and kissed me again. I was going to need an oxygen tank soon.

"Save it for the bedroom," I heard my dad shout from the entrance, and it was the equivalent of dousing me in cold water. I pulled away and caught my breath.

"You have my attention. What about last night?" I asked as reality set in. I was kissing Jax. I would be the other woman if things kept going.

"I am a fool," Jax replied in a softened tone, resting his forehead on mine.

"Okay, I can agree with that. I like where this conversation is going. What else you got for me?" I smirked.

"God, Candy, I love it when your eyes dance for me. It makes me feel like I am the only man in your life." He pulled back from me. "I am so angry with you, but I can't say goodbye to you, Candy. I will never be able to say goodbye, but I can't let you hurt me, either. I want you to go home because it is not safe for either one of us if you stay."

There was the double-edged sword. Jax wanted me in his life, but only if there was some guarantee he wouldn't get hurt. I couldn't blame him. He had every right to be as pissed as he was the night before. I wouldn't have blamed him if he'd have stayed gone.

I nodded my understanding, even if I had none. I didn't want to think about what my actions had done, so I grabbed his hand and smiled.

"Hungry?" I asked.

"Starving." Jax winked, and I squeezed his hand and led him back into the restaurant to enjoy my birthday breakfast.

Five hours passed as we hogged all the seats in the restaurant. I didn't care. I was with the people I loved most, and one person who would need Jenny Craig after I was done with her. Mark, Jax, and my dad excused themselves to go to the bathroom at the same time Brooklyn, Christina, and I headed to one as well. Michelle and Andrew were in deep conversation, so we left them to it.

Christina was changing the baby when I got done and I rushed through washing my hands, so there was no awkward conversation between us. I won't lie and say it wasn't nice to see she was doing well. I wanted the best for her, for everyone in my life.

"Candice, do you still hate me?" Christina asked, as I reached for the handle to exit the bathroom. I sighed. I had wanted to avoid this.

"Look, I am happy you have Chelle. I am happy you seem to be happy. I want the world for you, but if I were you I would never trust me to be alone in a room with you. If there wasn't a baby and a witness in this bathroom your face would most likely be rearranged with my fist."

"Candice, for what it's worth, I am sorry I hurt you. I miss you," Christina whispered, as Brooklyn walked out of a stall to wash her hands.

I pulled the door handle and left one conversation to hear another I probably shouldn't have.

"Jaxson, when are you going to tell her?" my dad asked.

"I'm not," he said.

"You cannot be serious. She has a right to know. Did you at least come clean about who Vanessa is?"

"No. Look, the bottom line is Candice needs to go home before she gets hurt."

I sucked in a breath and slid down the wall to crouch on the floor.

"Brooklyn will tell her if you don't. They have some kind of mutual women's flower power thing. You need to be honest and tell her." Mark spoke in a low, stern tone.

"If you put a ring on this woman while Candice is here, that would send her home, but it would kill her as well," my dad said, and I gripped my chest. *A ring?* I couldn't believe he would propose to this woman when he just had his tongue down my throat.

Christina emerged from the bathroom and didn't even see me as she headed to the table. I wish I could have said the same for Brooklyn, who slid down the wall beside me, as the men continued talking around the corner from us.

"I am going to give her a ring, but Candice is not going to know," Jax said. Brooklyn took my hand in hers and gave it a little squeeze.

"You're a fool. How do you plan to explain that little incident on the street?" Mark asked.

"I will figure it out," Jax replied.

"My daughter loves you, Jaxson. If she ever finds out, she will never forgive you." My dad's voice was soft, tinged with exhaustion.

"I know," Jax replied, sounding defeated.

"I hope you know what you are doing and that you end this with her soon," Mark said, and they walked out of the bathroom.

All three looked down to see me sitting with Brooklyn, eavesdropping on their conversation. We were busted, but I didn't care anymore.

Mark stuck out his arm and helped Brooklyn up as I stared at Jax. I couldn't keep my eyes from watering. I truly wanted to be happy for him, but I couldn't be. Mark helped me up and I turned to my dad. He wouldn't even look at me.

I brushed past them all and said my apologies and farewells to everyone else. I then ran out the door and grabbed a cab. I contemplated heading straight for the airport, but that is what I did last time. This time I wouldn't stick my head in the sand.

"Take me to Roosevelt Island."

Chapter Thirteen

I loved Roosevelt Island. I climbed over the miniature wall that surrounded the lighthouse, just like I had a thousand times before, and sat on a rock to watch the water lap against the shore. Then I made a wish.

"I wish that whatever is supposed to happen in my life would get on with it, because I keep getting stuck in my emotions and I am not happy here. I wish I could let go of Chase and leave him to rest in peace. I wish I could stop thinking of torturous weight gaining techniques for Christina. Most of all, I wish that if Jax and I were meant to be together then we would be, and if not, then I wish I could just let go."

I picked up a rock and threw it into the water. It skipped across the surface as the sun shone on the ripples. I saw the clouds rolling in that were supposed to bring more rain, if not snow. I laid back on the rocks and closed my eyes.

"Candy." I heard Chase's voice in my imagination. I looked up at the sky and felt a chill in the air. I believed his spirit was with me. I wanted to believe he was telling me it was all right to move on. I needed to hear those words from someone who could no longer talk. I saw the little bit of sun peek through the clouds and my brain wanted me to believe that it was Chase's pathway to heaven. I closed my eyes again and stayed beside the water.

"Candice?" I heard Jax and opened my eyes. To my surprise, the sun was setting and there was thunder in the distance.

"Are you engaged?" I asked, and the silence said it all. "I am trying to be happy for you, but it's really hard."

"Candy, it's not what you think," he replied, exhaling heavily.

"I am not dumb, Jax. I see the photos online. I was in your house when she was trying to check you for strep throat with her tongue. I saw the way you looked happy when you spoke to her on the phone. It is exactly what I think. My only question is why? Why wouldn't you just leave me to hate you and move on?"

Jax climbed over the wall and lay down beside me on the rocks.

"This is really uncomfortable," he muttered.

"The conversation or the rocks?" I asked.

"The rocks." He got up, then held out his hands to me, lifting me to my feet. I stared into the water as he wrapped his arms around me from my back. I rested against his chest, leaning my head on his shoulder.

"It's not what you think, Candice. I need you to trust me. Things aren't as they seem," he whispered.

"Jax, this isn't one of the books I write. I won't be the other woman, so save the lies and bullshit for someone who doesn't know better."

"Vanessa's brother killed Chase," Jax whispered, and I tried to spin and slap him, but he held me tightly. "Before you turn all *WWE Diva* on me, I need you to listen."

I paused and thought about it for a second. If I heard him out, he would most likely let me go and then I could assault him. Sounded plausible, so I nodded.

"Our last piece of Intel said Vanessa's older brother, known as Alejandro, and her younger brother, Niko, fled to Columbia to restart the organization there. We have no photos of the older brother, only a description. I started dating her to get him to come out. If I put a ring on her finger, her family has to come out. Enough time has passed that he would believe she is truly engaged." Jax held me tight.

"Does Vanessa know she is being used?" I asked softly.

"No. She believes this is a real relationship."

"So you take her on dates, tell her you love her, and make love to her, but it's not real? This is better than the stuff my brain created to write in books." I started fighting him again. Mark's words came back to me about how Jax was balls deep in a case. He wasn't lying, but I took it as metaphorical and not literal.

"Listen to me! I love you, Candice. It's you I want to marry. It's you I want to spend my life with. It has always been you. Damn it, woman, stop fighting me and listen to me!"

I stopped trying to get loose, and took a deep breath, exhaling loudly so he would know I was trying to calm down.

"My world revolves around the very thought of you. I would marry you this very minute, if I knew you could put Chase behind you," he whispered.

My heart melted at his words, but something told me this moment was not going to be all hearts and flowers. It would not be the romantic tale I would put in a book because we had both hurt each other.

"Jax—"

"You include Chase in everything you do and say whether you mean to or not. Whether you want to admit it or not, you had him in bed with us that night. I can't compete with him, because he is no longer here. I can't fight to get your heart because only you can get it back from him. I want to be with you more than my next breath, but I can't go through what happened last time. My focus here and now is catching Chase's killer."

I took a deep breath and looked at the water. I decided to let go and let life lead me. Whatever happened from here on out would be because it was meant to happen. But I had to leave him with a better memory of me than the one he got last time.

"Jax, it's my birthday and you didn't get me a gift, so for my present...would you come back to the hotel with me? I just need you to stay with me for a while. I miss how the three of us used to just sit and hang out together. I want that tonight. I just want a perfect night with my friend and then tomorrow I will fly back home."

Jax let me go and placed his hand on the small of my back to lead me to the waiting cab. We climbed inside and headed toward the hotel. His phone began ringing and he glanced at it and turned it off. I knew it was her, but was grateful I didn't have to hear their friendly banter. I laid my head on Jax's shoulder and suddenly felt at home with him again. In the physical sense it was as if nothing had happened, but emotionally we were battered and bruised. Somehow, I knew we would come out all right.

Upon entering my hotel room, my cell phone started ringing. I picked it up and didn't recognize the number, so I silenced it and left it on the counter. I ditched my coat and vest along with my boots. Then I turned on the television and we cuddled. It was like before, when Chase was alive and we would watch a movie together. I would curl up on Jax as Chase gave me a foot rub to appease me for whatever he had done wrong.

"Jax, do you really love me?" I asked over a re-run of *The Big Bang Theory*.

"More than my own life," he replied, and I looked up at him. I stared into his eyes looking for a lie or something that said he wasn't being honest, but his eyes said he loved me.

I thought about my earlier actions and where they had led me, but I wanted his warmth. I wanted his comfort, but most of all I wanted to feel his love. I climbed up him and placed my lips on his warm, soft mouth. Jax pulled me down into his arms and held me in his lap as he kissed me back with the heat of a raging fire. I threaded my fingers through his silky brown hair.

I pulled away breathlessly and climbed off him, then stood up and took his hand. I led him into the bedroom.

"Candice," Jax said, but I put my finger over my lips and climbed up on the bed. "Candice what are you doing?"

"We can either jump on the bed like children or rock it like adults!"

I rose and pulled my shirt off exposing my white lace bra. Then, in a sultry dance, I pulled my pants off to reveal my white lace panties. Jax hit play on the dock and "Pour Some Sugar On Me" by Def Leppard came on.

I dropped to my knees and flung my hair back. I rubbed my hands all over my body while Jax watched and his manhood tried to bust through his zipper. I slid my index finger into my mouth and sucked on it as my hips rocked back and forth. Then I took that finger and ran it down my body and into my panties.

Jax reached out and stopped me. His pupils were dilated and his breathing erratic. I smirked at him.

"Did you want to jump on the bed like toddlers?" I asked.

"No."

"Do you want to rock the bed with me?"

"Before I answer that, are you sure you want to do this? Are you sure you want me with you, knowing I am going to go back to Vanessa when it's over?"

"Jax, I am letting life lead me this time. It led me to you, now I want you in this bed with me. When we're done, life will lead us where we need to go. If it's together, great. If not, then at least we will both know we love each other. Even if we don't wind up together, I want to know someone out there loves me." I pulled him toward me by his pants.

"I don't care if you call out *Santa Claus* when you orgasm. You don't ever run from me again. You always tell me you are leaving and give me the opportunity to try to stop you!"

I nodded my agreement as I pulled his holster off and set it on the nightstand. By the time I returned to unbutton his pants, he had flipped me on my back and was climbing over me in a rush.

He pulled off his shirt and then pinned my hands above my head and laid on top of me. He kissed my neck and I writhed with need under him. I could feel his heart beating against mine.

His tongue made a hot velvet sweep against my lips as I gave him entry into my mouth. My blood raced under my skin as my body heated up. I moaned into his mouth and he swallowed it and kissed me again. My hips undulated under him as I tried to get some pressure on the apex between my thighs from his jeans, but he lifted up, so it left me needy and whiny.

"You taste like strawberries," Jax whispered, as he moved to my collarbone with sweeps of his tongue. I was going to respond, but he took my breath from me when he sucked my nipple through my bra into his mouth without warning. My body arched off the bed as he held my hands. I wiggled and squirmed with need. I tried to rub my thighs together, but he had put himself between my legs.

"Please!" I begged and Jax looked up at me. "We have had twenty years of foreplay. Tonight, can you just get inside me, please? I feel like I am going to combust."

Jax chuckled and released my hands. I immediately leaped to my knees and kissed him senseless. I got him up on his knees as I unbuckled his pants and began pushing them down his toned ass. He grabbed my bra and panties and tore them off me as I moaned in response.

"Sweet as sugar, Candy Cane." Jax leaned forward and sucked my hardened bare nipple back into his warm mouth. I ran my hands through his hair and pulled him closer to me. He bit down on my nipple in a teasing manner and I wanted to scream, but bit my lip instead.

I pulled his hair back and tugged his face up to mine, kissing him again.

"We have all night, Candice. What's the rush?" Jax asked, as I pushed at his pants.

"We have all night for round two, round three, round four, and however many more rounds we can go. After yesterday and today, I just need you inside me. I need you to fill me with your rock hard cock. I need to know that, for this one fleeting moment in time, I am yours and you are mine."

Jax pulled his socks and shoes off as he pulled his pants off. He stood before me, his chest showed his muscles from his constant workout routine. His tanned skin reminded me of hot caramel, and made me want to weep at his sculpture-like physique.

Jax climbed up on the bed and laid down. He was allowing me to have what I wanted. I really wanted him to feel how frustrating he is at times. Foreplay has a time and place, but it wasn't here, tonight. I wanted to taste him, savor him, be filled by him.

I wrapped my hands around his large length and began to stroke him. As I moved my hand up and down his cock, I lowered my head until my tongue could reach out and swipe at the pre-cum atop his penis.

His flavor hit my tongue with a powerful punch. It was like tasting chocolate for the first time. I nipped at his stomach. Then I placed kisses lower and lower, moving my lips centimeter by centimeter down his chiseled abdomen. Jax placed his hand on my head and let out a frustrated groan that made me smile.

"Go lower," he ground out, as I kissed just above his shaft.

I then kissed the inside of his thigh and cupped his balls. I felt his hand tighten on my hair as I ran my tongue across his balls lightly, sucking them.

"Put me in your mouth, Candy," Jax groaned.

I decided to appease him. I licked the tip and then allowed my mouth to hollow out and flattened my tongue as I took him to my throat and swallowed.

"Christ, that's good!"

I smiled and continued on my up and down course on his cock. He groaned and gripped my head each time I swallowed. I pulled my hand up to follow my mouth because he was too large to get him completely in my mouth. I continued my stroking and swallowing until he was swelling inside my mouth.

"Candice, stop!" Jax begged. I pulled off his length with a pop from my mouth. "You ready to do this?" he asked.

"No," I replied and licked the rim of the head of his cock. I watched his body tense and his eyes roll back in his head, as I took him to the back of my throat again and swallowed a few more times, pulling him in and out while I watched him watch me. When he gripped the sheets with both fists, I pulled back off with a popping sound as he fell out of my mouth. I placed a lingering kiss on the crown and smiled.

"Now I am ready," I said with a smile, as Jax groaned at the loss of my mouth.

"You're going to kill me with that mouth, Candice."

I smiled and climbed up his body and placed my hands on his chest as he held himself under me. I leaned forward and kissed him slowly as I descended on his cock. Each agonizing inch made my body scream for more. I wanted to impale him, but this slow delicious torture was better than just jumping on.

I rose up and watched his face as I took him to the hilt. I bit my lip as I watched him staring into my eyes, his jaw clenched. I sat perfectly still and embraced the moment. I may not have Jax after tonight, but here and now I was reclaiming my love for him. My heart may not be whole, but what was left belonged to Jax and there was no doubt at this moment that we belonged to each other.

"Ride me, Candy. You know how good it is when I'm on top. Now show me what you got."

I sat back and began lifting myself up and down his length. I closed my eyes as I pulled him nearly out and stared into his eyes, moaning as I came back down. He filled me, hitting every spot that would make my skin turn to fire and my hue change to a rosy color, letting him know exactly what he was doing to me.

He held my hips to guide me into a rhythm that worked for us both. It was neither fast nor slow. It was deliciously perfect. I grabbed my breasts and kneaded them. Jax pulled my hands down, tugging me to him and sucking my nipple into his mouth. I moaned and lost my rhythm. Jax continued his onslaught of my nipple as he helped me get back to the delectable pace we had.

"Candy," Jax said. I looked down at him. "Relax your legs and spread them."

I did as he said and, as he sucked my nipple back into his mouth, he held my hips in place as he began to lift into me. I screamed as he got deeper inside me. I could feel him everywhere as I rode closer to orgasm. My toes curled as he put his hands on my face to bring me down for a kiss as I returned to riding him.

"Jax. You feel too good," I groaned, when he let me up for air.

"You were made for me. Let me feel you come on me."

I whimpered as I closed my eyes. I was so close and he had swollen inside me, so I could feel nothing but him. He had invaded my mind, body, soul, and taken over my heart. This orgasm was going to take my breath away.

"Say it, Jax. Tell me!" I moaned, sitting up to watch him as neared climax.

"I love you, Candice!"

"Jax!" I called out, as I clamped down on him. He took over pushing into me as I screamed his name over and over.

"Look at me!" he demanded, as my body combusted, and tried to pull him in deeper as the waves of my orgasm rolled through me.

"I love you, Jax!" I shouted, as I vibrated around his hardened cock, trying to ride the last of my orgasm.

I stared down into his eyes as my breath was stolen from me. I watched as his face tightened as he slammed into me. I heard the groan as he found his release. He gritted his teeth and continued to pump into me after his seed was already flowing out.

I collapsed against him. He brushed my hair off my face as we both breathlessly felt the aftershocks. I had tried to fight it. I tried to run from it. I tried to deny it, but the truth was I loved Jax. I still wondered if it was disrespecting Chase, but I couldn't ignore it anymore. I couldn't after I saw him with Vanessa.

"Want some water?" I asked and he nodded as he caught his breath. I climbed off and stepped onto the floor where his semen dripped out of me.

"That has to be the sexiest thing I have ever seen."

"What is?" I asked with a hoarse voice, as I stood naked in front of him.

"To see part of me coming from inside you," Jax muttered with a smirk that spoke volumes of what he was thinking.

I grabbed two of the cups and headed to the bathroom to fill them with water. I looked up in the mirror after filling them to see Jax behind me. I turned to hand him his water, and he downed it on the spot. He threw the plastic cup over his shoulder and missed the trash can as he came toward me with a predatory look.

I held my hand up to stop him as I slowly sipped my water. He groaned and I smiled behind my cup as I took another sip. He walked over and turned on the shower. I watched him grab the towels as I took each drop in deliberate measure, to extend my time to make him sweat. I closed my eyes as the water flowed in the background and I held water in my cup and made another wish on the water.

I wish this is what my life could be like. I wish that Chase would find peace with me being with Jax. I wished for him to leave Vanessa, knowing he wouldn't until Chase's killer was brought to justice, or until an eye for an eye was dealt. I knew Jax well enough to know what he intended to do when he found him.

I was at the close of my wish when I felt hands take my cup and then within a second I was tossed over the shoulder of a six-foot muscled man who wanted me in the shower with him.

"Put me down," I playfully squealed, as he walked into the shower.

"How about I put you down on me. You did promise a round two." He planted me against the wall.

"You can have all the rounds you want when you look at me like I am the only woman in the world," I said, as he went for my neck and the water cascaded down his tanned muscular back.

"You are the only woman in the world who catches my attention."

Just like that, round two had begun and round four wouldn't end until well after the sun came up. We were never sated. It was never enough. I craved his energy as he craved my body. I refused to let guilt ruin what felt so right. I hoped he was part of my life's plan.

Chapter Fourteen

"Jax, do you think Chase is happy?" I asked as I twirled my fingers down his sculpted chest. I was lying in the crook of his shoulder on the bed we had just made love in.

"I think he misses you. I know I would miss you. I think he will be happy when he sees you are happy."

Jax turned his head and planted a kiss on the top of my head. I closed my eyes and reveled in the intimacy of the moment. Soon this would be over. I would be on a plane home and Jax would be putting a ring on Vanessa's finger.

"I want him to be all right with us being together," I said, immediately noticing the look Jax gave me that reminded me we were not together. "What I mean is, if we could be together, how would we know he was all right with it? How will I know when I am ready to let him go?"

Jax sat up and I came up with him. He reached down off the bed and grabbed his wallet from his jeans.

"You know we didn't use a condom," he muttered under his breath.

"I'm on the pill," I replied, watching him open his wallet.

"Why?" Jax asked, halting what he was doing.

"Why what?"

"Why are you on the pill? Are you sleeping with someone?" He spoke softly, but his tone told a tale of anger and bitterness.

"No, it's to regulate my period. Are you trying to start a fight?" I responded with unease.

"No, but what's mine is mine and you are mine. I don't care about what happened before we walked in here last night. I care about what happens after. I want to get so deep inside you, that you are ruined for anyone else. I want to make you come so hard my name is the only name you yell. I want to entrap your heart in mine, so no one else can have it. I want you to be mine."

Jax leaned in and kissed me, letting his lips lightly brush mine. Then he pulled back and opened his wallet. I was essentially speechless. What could I say to a heartfelt statement when I know he would be in bed with another woman by dinner?

Jax pulled out a folded-up piece of paper. It looked like it had been read a thousand times and was barely holding itself together. He placed it in my hand and stood up. I looked at him in question, but he merely nodded at the letter, almost as if it could speak for itself.

I watched as he closed the curtains. The sun was up and so was our time together. In a few hours, this would be a memory to hold close to my heart. I could yell and scream and demand that he leave Vanessa. I know he would if I asked him to, but he would always regret Chase's killer going free. I had to be adult enough to let him find closure and justice.

"I am going to call room service. Want anything?" he asked.

"Waffles. I love waffles." I opened the letter. The first place I looked was at the bottom to see Chase's name. I inspected the writing and knew it was his. Then I read it.

Jaxson,

You are my partner, my best friend, and the only person I can trust some days. We have been to hell and back over the years, and I honestly wouldn't have made it as far as I did without you. I don't have much to say because you already know it all. So instead of a confessional goodbye, I want to ask a favor of you in regards to Candice.

Take her in your arms and love her like I know you do. She is stubborn, so give her time to breathe and then hold her when she cries. Keep her safe in your arms as I should have done. Marry her and never let her get away. The world is cruel and I don't want her looking for love in it when you have loved her for years. Make babies with her and name one after me. But most importantly, make her happy, love her, and let her be set free from me.

If you could do these things I ask, I will be forever in your debt. Keep an eye on Christina, too. I am sure my family has taken her in with the baby on the way, but I want my child to be well cared for. Visit my baby weekly and help turn it into the kind of person I was. You were the best brother I could have I love you.

Chase

I crushed the letter to my chest and a tear fell from my eye. All this time I had been carrying around guilt for doing exactly what Chase wanted. I had become a victim of my own way of thinking. I had hurt so many in an attempt to be free.

Jax returned and sat on the bed, pulling me into his arms. I cried on his chest.

"I am so sorry, Jax," I murmured over and over again.

I turned my head and placed my teardrop covered lips on his. Jax kissed me back as though it was the first time he had ever kissed me. I opened my mouth and allowed him entry, his flavor hitting me in a rush as our tongues tangled together. There was an overwhelming taste of coffee in his mouth.

I turned my body to face him, threading my hand through his silky hair as I spread my legs to straddle him. Jax moved back on the bed and I followed and then sank onto his shaft as my wetness coated my thighs. I would never get enough of this. I would never have enough time with him.

Jax pulled me close and kissed my neck as I coaxed myself up and down his hardened length. This was not lovemaking, this was raw and carnal. This was intimate and erotic love in the most basic form. My heart was his, and he was gifting me with the same.

I leaned back to allow him to take my nipple into his mouth and I moaned. I reached behind me and cupped his balls and massaged them in my hand. My reward was a sharp thrust inside me to that rough patch behind my pelvic bone. My moisture coated him and I was lost in the heat of the moment.

Jax reached down in front to find the tight bundle of nerves my folds were hiding and stroked my clit until I was panting his name. He urged me up the cliff to my climax.

"Jax." I moaned, and then I bit down on his shoulder as I screamed when my body turned to fire and burned with each orgasmic wave.

I was sore and tired, but he wasn't done. I watched as the man who owned my heart pushed into me as if trying to climb inside. I gritted my teeth as I swelled from my first orgasm while feeling the second one stirring. My body would explode like a volcano and I would be left as nothing but ash.

I watched as Jax turned into an alpha and seemed to be trying to claim me as his. I had read about it in books, but he didn't have that style until now. He was marking me with his manhood to keep others away. He tugged on my hair and my head fell back as he bit down on my nipple. I screamed with the overload of sensation.

"Say my name," Jax groaned, as he swelled inside me.

"Jax!" I screamed, and tried to tighten down on him to make it more intense for us both. It didn't take long before I was chanting his name and my body exploded in sensual bliss. A few pumps later and Jax found his release and kissed me when he came. I leaned my head onto his shoulder and tried to catch my breath. My legs were tingly and my body trembled as I came down from my high.

I heard the knock on the door, but neither of us moved to get it. I stayed sitting on him and we cuddled in the afterglow of orgasmic bliss. There was nothing to be said. We merely knew that our time was ending. I would go back to California and Jax would return to Vanessa. I had hope. I would wish on the water that if he found the man responsible, he would come back for me.

"Leave it at the door," Jax called out, as the knock sounded again.

I slowly pulled up and felt a loss as soon as he slid out of me. My legs were weak, so Jax helped me into the shower. The warm water cascaded down my body as he soaped up every inch of me. Then he rinsed me while adding kisses to my neck and shoulder.

I giggled at the ticklish sensation he left after each kiss. Then he turned me around and began shampooing my hair. A girl could get used to this. I had never had anyone do this for me before. It was invigorating. My body tingled and goosebumps rose all over my body with each touch. Then he turned me back around and placed me under the water.

In a slow, methodical movement, he rinsed my hair as my head tilted back and he kissed my exposed neck. As soon as I thought we were tired, one of us was ready to go again. I reached forward and took his long cock into my hand and coaxed it back and forth, feeling the hardened silk come to life in my hands.

I dropped to my knees, pulling him into my mouth and took him in as far as I could, then swallowed down on him. I cupped his length and set a relentless pace to bring him to orgasm. The water flowed down his body and into my face, but I didn't care where my next breath came from when I heard him groan and grab my hair.

I needed to taste him more than I needed my next breath. I needed every experience with him. I wanted to take him to the zoo on a real date and have him read to me in the library like we used to. I wanted to walk around the lake we grew up by. I wanted him to hold me and never let me go, but I understood that he needed to do this for Chase, that catching this killer had become his top priority in my absence.

Jax tried to pull me up off of him, and I only sucked him harder. He gripped my head when I grabbed his toned ass, letting him know I wasn't going anywhere. I felt him swell and hollowed out my cheeks, and flattened my tongue to let him take charge.

He pumped in and out of my mouth as I swallowed down each time he hit the back of my throat. His movements became sporadic as he swelled. I tightened my grip on him so he couldn't pull away. I saw his head go back as he groaned. The first spurt was thick and I swallowed it immediately. I practically inhaled his flavor and memorized it, so I would never forget the way it tasted. Then I licked him clean.

"Your turn," Jax said, as I climbed to my feet.

"No, that was so whenever you're with another woman, *my* name is the one you will call."

Jax smiled and I laughed as we finished showering. I soaped him up, making sure to rub those overly sensitive places over and over again. He thought he could brand me with his penis and he had, but I had done the same with my mouth and my pussy.

We exited the shower and Jax grabbed the terry cloth robe and donned it as he wrapped a large white fluffy towel around me. He took my hand and another towel and brought me out to the bed. He picked me up like a bride and sat me on the edge as he took the other towel and climbed behind me to dry my hair.

I was in Heaven. I remembered the last time someone was this attentive. It was right before Chase had gone undercover, and changed our lives forever. With the memory in my head, for once I didn't break down into tears. I didn't feel guilty that I was here with Jax.

I would never find peace with what happened, but I had learned to cope with it. I could only hope he was smiling down on us from Heaven. I was so smitten and relaxed that my brain didn't even focus on the ringing of my phone until Jax put it in front of me.

"Hello," I answered.

"Are you coming to work today or are you going to keep running off?" Andrew asked.

"I will be late, but I will be there. I wanted to talk to you when you have time."

"I have time now. We definitely need to talk about your job, and I have your coffee," Andrew replied, and it seemed like whatever had been bothering him the other night was gone. That irritation in his voice had been replaced with concern.

"I'm sorry, Andrew. I am just getting up. This resetting my clock to the east coast has screwed with me." I was lying, but I didn't want him here with Jax.

"Are you sure it is your clock that has you messed up and not whoever will be drinking the second cup of coffee on the tray outside your door?"

I was essentially busted unless I could think of a creative lie. I don't know why I was hiding Jax from Andrew. Maybe because I didn't want anyone to know, or maybe I didn't want to be the steak that two dogs fight over.

"It's my coffee. I ordered two so I can have one now and bring one to the conference room," I said, hoping he wouldn't pry.

"Is Mark in there with you?" Andrew asked.

"No, why would Mark be here?"

"Just a hunch from the way Mark followed when you took off after that kiss from Jaxson."

"No, that kiss was old friends saying goodbye. As far as Mark, there is nothing there. I think he is with Brooklyn," I rebutted, and Jax came to stand in front of me. He shook his head, as if to say *no more*. Then he pushed the speaker button on my phone to hear.

"If Mark is with Brooklyn then wouldn't that be a conflict of interests of their cases?" Andrew pried. Jax glared at the phone. There was something I wasn't following happening here.

"Andrew, I am flying home tonight. Being here was a mistake. If you give me half an hour, I will meet you at the conference room."

"Is it a mistake because Jax is working your dead fiancé's case? I heard them saying it would be hard for you and him when it was all put to rest."

"Andrew, I need to get ready. I will be down in half an hour." I spoke quickly and hung up.

"What the hell was that? Who has he been around?" Jax asked, pulling his jeans on.

"I don't know. I left him at dinner with Mark and Brooklyn. Then I left him at breakfast with everyone. Maybe they talked about Chase."

"Mark and Brooklyn never discuss cases with anyone outside of the case." Jax gritted his teeth in anger.

I watched in silence as he pulled his phone out and turned it on. I felt his playful, loving mood fade away. I felt my heart evaporating into nothing. Our time was up and it would be hard, but I would go home and cyber stalk him. I might sign Vanessa up for a chocolate of the month club as a wedding present. As immature as it was, if she got fat I think I would be happier.

Within a half hour, Jax and I were both dressed and practically ignoring each other. Mark and Brooklyn were in my hotel living room. They were carrying on a conversation about who did what, where and how. I wasn't listening, because I finally had something to write about. I was getting lost in the story as the world faded in the background.

I opened my laptop and started writing my next novel. I usually begin with a name and a plot, but this one was coming from the heart. The name would come last and the plot would happen based on what the characters needed instead of what I planned. I was going to let life lead me. As I stared at the white screen, I had my first chapter done. I decided there was something I needed to do. I picked up my phone and texted Andrew.

You will have my resignation in your email. I can't be what you need me to be. I am a writer. I always have been. I'm sorry.

I didn't get a response as the hours flew by. By the time I stopped writing to order coffee, the sun had set and everyone had gone. I even missed my flight. I would have to catch a flight in the morning. I saw a note on the phone and lifted it to read it.

Candy,

You were busy so I tried not to bother you. I hope to see you before you leave. If not, know that I will love you as long as the water in your wishes flows.

Jax

Chapter Fifteen

I heard a knock and lifted my head off the desk in my hotel room. I must have fallen asleep. I looked at the clock—five in the morning. I got up to go climb in the bed for another hour before heading to the airport when I heard another knock.

When I opened the door, Jax was standing there in his denim jeans, black boots and a black button-down shirt, wearing a smile. I smiled brightly, excited to see him.

"Get dressed, beautiful. I am taking you somewhere." Jax ushered me into the room to get me dressed.

"Where are we going?" I asked, as curiosity revved my writer's brain.

"It's a secret," he whispered with a smile.

"I can keep a secret."

"That's good, but I am keeping mine."

"How will I know what to wear if I don't know where we are going?" I asked, my bottom lip extending into a sulky pout. Jax ignored it and went to the dresser, pulling out a pair of skinny jeans, a blue, off the shoulder sweater, and my black Uggs. He handed them over with a smile that said *problem solved.*

I got dressed and put on my thick winter coat. Then we rode down the elevator, hand in hand. I was so excited, yet I knew nothing about what was happening. He ushered me out the front door and into a waiting cab.

The driver immediately left and no one told him where to go. My writer's brain went on auto-pilot as the plot thickened. I noticed the winds were whipping at the car and imagined we were going to kill zombies in a graveyard or even something creepier that would make Stephen King proud.

That was my next goal. I would write something that was romantic, yet creepy and weird, but addicting. Maybe one day he would give me a quote for my cover. That would be impressive, because I don't often see his name giving quotes on covers. I watched as we crossed the river and Jax squeezed my hand.

"Are you going to tell me where we are going?" I asked, and Jax merely shook his head. He pulled me over to him and I curled into his chest, throwing my legs over his legs. I didn't care where we went when I was enveloped in the strength and warmth that came from just being near him.

We pulled up outside of the northern tip of our river as the clouds rumbled and tried to hide the rising sun. Jax opened the door and pulled me out of the cab. He walked me over to our lighthouse, where I looked over and saw the river churning where it met the ocean. I watched as the winds carried the waves up over portions of the lighthouse.

"I wanted you to see that your wishes are heard. They are trying to tell you they are listening. It's time you make a wish to beat all your other wishes. It's time to wish for yourself. Just you this time, instead of including everyone else."

I closed my eyes as Jax wrapped his arms around me from behind me. I listened as the sky purred from a cold front moving in to bring more snow. I could hear the waves crashing against the wall and felt the splatter of water drops on my face.

I didn't need to wish on the water. I had everything I needed right there at that very moment. With the completion of my next book, I could get my publisher back. I could go home to California and have my dad come and visit me more. I could always come back to New York to visit him as I didn't feel the need to hide anymore.

I still hated Christina. Not for what they had done by making baby Chelle, but because they hid it from everyone for months out of Chase's selfish need to keep me in his life and in the dark. I would exact my revenge by making her a character who gets maimed in one of my books.

The only thing I wanted, I was letting go of because I needed him to get the same closure I had found. Jax would need to find a way to cope like I had. My grieving sent me across the country. Jax's grieving is sending him to hunt down the guilty party. I knew it wouldn't bring Chase back and when it was all over Jax wouldn't feel any better, but he would have to figure that out for himself.

"Jax, I don't have anything to wish for," I whispered as I opened my eyes and watched the waves slam against the concrete wall. It was amazing to see the water come to life as the storm blew in. I turned my head to the side and looked up at Jax, who planted a kiss on my lips.

Then he let go and turned me to face him. He got down on one knee and my hands flew to my open mouth.

"Candice-Leigh Carson, I want you to wear this ring as a promise that you will wait for me. What has happened over the last few months doesn't matter, because the truth is I have been waiting for you for over twenty years. No one else has my heart. It is yours. It has always been yours. Before you get on a plane and leave me again, take this ring and my heart with you."

Jax slid the ring over my finger as my hands trembled with emotion.

"I promise to come for you when this is all over," he continued. "I promise to love you and protect you. I promise to wipe your tears away and hold you tight. I promise to make love to you every night and take you to every lighthouse in the world. I promise to make you believe in me as I believe in you. I promise to be the best friend that you deserve. I promise I will be a husband who will make you proud. I promise you everything I can give you. I promise you me."

My heart fluttered and my eyes grew moist. He wasn't proposing, but he was asking me to wait for him. I nodded as tears of joy flowed. He stood and lifted me off the ground to spin me around, as my voice echoed cheerful squeals.

He kissed me hard and deep as he sat me back down on the ground and my body instantly melted. I knew I loved Chase, but this is not how it felt with him. I would always love him and remember him, but what I had with Jax was growing stronger than anything I had felt before.

Jax pulled away breathlessly and we stared into each other's eyes. The winds had grown calm. The waters had stopped their assault on the wall. Jax took my left hand and pulled it up to show a beautiful princess cut diamond with a frame of diamonds around it onto my finger. It was at least a carat or more. It must have cost him a fortune.

"It's beautiful," I whispered, as my emotions overflowed.

"You're beautiful." Jax pulled me to him for another kiss. As our lips locked, I felt something wet touch my face. Then another splash hit my hand. I pulled back and looked around to see the waves had calmed and the snow had come.

Maybe Jax had been right that the waves were churning my wishes to make them come true. I know our relationship was not one of fairy tales, but that is what made it mean more. No one wants to be with someone they never fight with. I wanted someone I could fight with and make up with. I wanted someone who, when I went crazy and ran away, would stay home and wait for me to come to my senses. I wanted Jax.

We watched the snow for about twenty minutes and just enjoyed being with each other. Then we took the cab back to the hotel.

I took Jax's hand as we entered the elevator and pulled his arm to me and leaned my head against him. He placed a kiss on my head and the doors opened to my hallway.

When we arrived in the room, I barely got the door open before I was lifted off my feet. He carried me in, and my back hit the wall behind me as Jax held me with his hip and tore off my jacket. I pulled off his jacket as he went for my neck.

I moaned and flung my head back into the wall, but didn't care. I lifted my sweater, exposing my black bra. I threw my shirt as Jax kissed my collarbone. Then he carried me over to the next wall, where there was an entryway table.

He shoved the picture frame and plant onto the floor and placed me on the table. He went to his knees and removed my shoes as I unbuttoned my pants. I lifted my body as he pulled my pants and underwear down and threw them across the entryway.

He pulled me to the edge and pushed my legs apart. I leaned back and gave him access, as his tongue immediately penetrated my entrance. I moaned and squirmed as he held my thighs in place.

I grabbed his brown hair and pulled him into me and then pushed him away; nothing would budge him. I gripped the entryway table as my orgasm came out of nowhere and slammed into me like a bat hitting a ball. My orgasm had knocked me out of the park.

Jax wasted no time standing up, as he slid his finger inside me, while he unlatched his pants and let them fall to the floor. He pulled his finger out and I whimpered with the loss. Then he picked me up and placed me back against the wall and pushed into me, as I continued to ride the waves of orgasmic bliss.

My fingers curled into his shoulder and I bit his neck, as he pushed into me hard and deep. He was literally everywhere and at the angle I was positioned, I was soaking us both.

"Oh God!" I screamed as he pushed into me harder.

"My name." Jax pushed harder.

"Jax!" I screamed and tried to climb away, as this orgasm was going to steal my soul.

"Where are you going?" Jax asked with a groan. He lifted my legs just enough that I was screaming until I went hoarse, as the ecstasy invaded every pore.

"I love you, Candy," Jax groaned, before he leaned down and shoved his tongue in my mouth. This was not lovemaking, this was taking possession of my body and soul.

"I love you, Jax," I called out with a hoarse voice, as I clawed and scratched at him. The electricity started in my belly and I tightened down as it spread like wildfire across every nerve ending. Then fireworks exploded in my body.

I stared into those gray eyes with hints of blue and saw waves of water crashing in my head, as I was lifted into an out-of-body moment of ecstasy. Then I lost my voice as I tumbled back to earth and shattered as Jax continued to pump into me. It wasn't much longer before he groaned my name and found his release.

He leaned over and placed a kiss on my forehead while we both struggled to catch our breath. He slowly lifted me off him and I instantly missed his length inside of me. He put me back on my feet and we got dressed.

"It always gets better and more intense with you," I whispered, as I waited for my voice to return.

"I was thinking the same thing about you," Jax murmured, as he urged me toward the shower. We both took a cup of water and downed it, throwing away the cups, missing the basket entirely. We laughed about it and Jax turned on the water. "Round two?" he asked, and I smiled.

A loud noise that sounded as though it came from the living room could be heard over the running water. Jax and I looked at each other and waited. Someone was knocking on the door to the hotel room.

"Jax, how did you know I was still here?" I asked, as I contemplated who else was aware I hadn't left. Something about the knock set my writer's brain into overdrive. My nerves tingled and I was no longer feeling the orgasmic bliss.

Questioning it relaxed me. It wasn't as if someone was breaking in, just knocking.

"Since you quit your job, I paid your hotel bill for today. If you checked out before your flight they were to call me. I wanted to make sure I saw you before you left," Jax said as he fastened his pants.

He went to the door and opened it. Christina was there, wearing pajama pants and a sweater with a coat. She was fidgeting and looking down at the floor.

"I was hoping you were here. Can we talk privately?" Christina asked, and Jax looked at me. I nodded, although I questioned her sanity in wanting to be alone with me when I still felt an overwhelming need to rearrange her face.

"I am going to go get coffee, and give you girls some time," Jax stated, then leaned down to place a kiss on my cheek before whispering, "I will arrest you if you kill her." I merely shook my head at him.

"How did you know I was still here?" I asked as he stepped out. "Why are you here? What is going on?"

Christina pulled out a letter, written on a small piece of paper, clear and precise. I noticed her hand shaking as she handed it to me, and her breathing seemed labored.

DELIVER JAXSON MONROE UNDER THE QUEENSBORO BRIDGE AND YOUR BABY WILL BE SAFE

"Do they have Chelle?" I asked trying to remain calm, but my heart sped as I thought about what might happen.

Christina paced in my hotel bedroom.

"No, she is fine. Your dad and Michelle took her to the Hamptons this morning because of the note," Christina muttered.

I sat and consoled her for about half an hour. I still had my issues and anger about what she had done, but this was above that. I put all those bitter feelings aside and became the friend I used to be.

She sent some texts and messed with her phone as we waited for Jax to return, so we could show him the note. I knew in the back of my mind that we should have called him that moment, but my heart said to wait another second, another minute, another hour even. The moment the note was presented to him I would have to say goodbye and be left on my own waiting for him. It was selfish to wait and I suddenly knew why Chase hid what he had done from me.

A knock sounded on the door, but this time it was as if someone was beating on the door with something heavy. Jax wouldn't knock like that.

"Am I interrupting something? Who is that?" Christina asked quietly.

"I don't know," I replied with a nervous twinge.

"Are we in danger?"

"I really don't think so, but it's better to be safe than sorry." I put a finger over my lips to tell her to be quiet.

The knock sounded again and this time I swore I heard wood fracture. I pulled out my phone and sent a group text message to Mark and Jax with one word: *Chase*. My stomach sank. I don't know why my writer's brain immediately thought we were about to be slaughtered, but it did.

Christina stood at the edge of the door of the closet as the doorframe of the main entrance shattered and Andrew walked in with Brent and two other men I had seen around our office.

"Andrew, what the hell?" I asked, and he looked me up and down and then gave me a murderous look.

"Where is he?" Andrew asked, as his green eyes glimmered.

"Who?" The other men began looking around the hotel room. I glanced at my broken door and knew something was very wrong. "You're scaring me, Andrew," I shouted, my voice hoarse.

"Did you scream because of his cock, or does the room always smell like sex?" Andrew snapped, ignoring my question. I looked behind me and Christina was getting ready to climb out of the back of the closet when I held my hand up behind my back to tell her not to.

"Andrew, please tell me what you want," I demanded, ignoring his earlier comment.

"I want your *boyfriend*." His words dripped with disdain at the term.

"I don't have a boyfriend," I replied, and then Andrew picked up my hand and looked at the ring that sparkled on my finger. He gave me a look that said he knew I was lying and tried to look past me. Then I took a step closer to him so he wouldn't see Christina. "Is this because we haven't taken our friendship out of the friend zone? Because, I have to tell you, breaking my door down is not how you get in my pants." I ran my finger down Andrew's chest.

Without warning, he picked me up by my throat and slammed me into the wall. I held my hand out to tell Christina not to move, that I would be fine. I closed my eyes and made a wish on the stars, the water, God, or whoever was listening to keep Jax away until this was over. I would rather die than have him walk into an ambush and lose him like I lost Chase.

"Listen, bitch!" Andrew hissed. "Tell your boyfriend he fucked up. He should have stayed out of my business and my family!"

Chapter Sixteen

When you think you are going to die, the only things you consider are the people who are most important to you. I thought about how Jax would probably be slaughtered the second he got back to the hotel, and how I had been the one who requested him to come in a text message. I would have led him to his own death.

I thought about my dad and wondered who would take care of him. I thought about Michelle and how she and Christina had learned to cope with a piece of Chase, but I was leaving nothing behind for anyone. I spent my whole life waiting for stuff to happen instead of making it happen.

My thoughts halted as dizziness invaded me. My air flow was being cut off. I would die with my hand out telling Christina to stay hidden. I may hate her, but no one deserved this. If Mark and Jax came in together, we might have a chance, but we couldn't survive on our own.

When Andrew allowed air into my lungs, I stared into his eyes. They were cold and heartless. There was nothing about this man that I knew. Everything had been a lie. He pressed in on my throat. I would surely wear bruises if I lived through this.

"You can tell him he is not the only one who's a great actor. He played my sister's boyfriend until she fell in love. I played your best friend until the time came to end him. I will end his life just like I did to the other one."

Andrew slowly allowed me down to my feet and let go of my throat. I immediately grabbed my throat as I gasped for air.

"You can tell him I will find him. And, when I do, you can bury him under the tree next to your other man."

I felt sick to my stomach. Out of the corner of my eye, I saw Christina had tears rolling down her face. Her hand was over her mouth and she was about to lose it when Andrew walked near the closet. I gathered up every ounce of energy I had to speak.

"Why?" I wheezed as I tried to control my coughing.

"They interfered where they shouldn't have. Make sure he goes to confession before I see him. You might want to mention that to your *boyfriend*." Andrew glared at me.

"I will tell him when I see him. Now get out!" I screamed, but it came out as a whisper.

"We will be watching you, sweetheart. Don't worry, though, I have seen enough of you to know that when you need a shoulder to cry on, we can pass you around like a bong. Isn't that how you met me, anyway? You needed a shoulder to cry on after you buried your fiancé and slept with his best friend. Seems like you enjoy being passed around."

Andrew snapped his fingers and the other men joined him and walked out of my broken door. I gasped for air, as Christina pried her way out of the closet and ran. So much for being a friend. I crawled forward and laid down on the floor.

"Candice?" Mark yelled, as I heard what was left of my door give way. "What the hell happened here?" He busted through, cleared the rooms and came for me. He put his gun back in its holster as he checked my pulse.

I tried as hard as I could to convey what had happened, but it didn't work. Jax barreled through the door with his gun drawn. As soon as he saw me, he enveloped me in his arms and rocked me. I swore I felt him crying.

I tried to talk, but the words wouldn't come. My throat burned with each attempt to verbalize anything. Mark brought me my laptop and I typed what had happened. While I could portray every detail and feeling there was only a sentence that needed to be said.

"Sweetheart, let's get you an ambulance," Mark said, inspecting my neck. I shook my head and held onto Jax with one arm, while typing slowly with one hand. It wouldn't take long to finish the story.

Andrew killed Chase, and is coming for Jax.

I passed the laptop to Mark who pulled his phone out and began placing calls. I was not worried about me, I was worried about Jax. This man wanted blood, and we already knew he was capable of it, because he had murdered Chase.

Jax lifted me off the floor carefully and placed me on the bed, as he read what I wrote. I watched as everything moved around me in slow motion. I concentrated when I saw a glow of light shine through the window. I imagined it was Chase who'd been keeping us safe. I imagined it was him watching over me. Then the light moved and I saw it was just another officer's badge shining off the reflection.

It was still snowing outside. I stared out the window while the police moved around my room. The hotel had called someone and they were repairing the frame and the door. For the rest of my stay I would have a guard at my door.

I was supposed to be flying home, but no one thought that was a viable plan. I was glad everyone said no, because I felt like if I left I would be leaving myself and Jax vulnerable. Together, we could fight. Separate, we would sink.

"Candice?" Brooklyn called from behind me and I turned to look at her with tears in my eyes. She gasped when I pulled my hand away and she could see the outline of finger prints on my throat. They were still a shade of scarlet, but as the blood settled beneath my skin, the bruises turned into a darkening purple.

"Candice, are you sure you don't want to go to the hospital?" Brooklyn asked, and I shook my head. Jax was safe here and doing his job. I was breathing, so there was really no reason to go. "At least let a medic check you," she begged, and I nodded. If it would help everyone, I would get checked.

They called for an ambulance and within ten minutes a medic was entering my room for me. The first medic came and felt my throat, shining a light in my mouth while the second checked my blood pressure. My respirations were fine and my voice was slowly coming back. I felt sore and my throat hurt, but it was nothing I couldn't handle. I could feel Jax watching me as the medic took my temperature. I looked up and met his eyes to see the guilt on his face.

I didn't want him to feel guilty. This was not his fault. I handed the thermometer back to the first medic, then marched over to Jax and went chest to chest with him. I wrapped my arms around him and laid my head against him.

"I should have been here. I should have stayed with you and Christina," Jax whispered.

"Where is Christina?" I said in a raspy voice.

"We are looking for her. She is one of us. We will find her. I am worried about you right now. Are you all right?" Jax pulled me back from him to look at the darkening bruises.

I wrapped my arms around his neck and brought his lips to mine. He barely kissed me back. I pulled back and glared at him.

"Kiss me like you mean it, or never kiss me at all!" I whispered as loudly as I could and Jax did just that. He grabbed me and lifted me off the floor as his velvety lips came down on mine. I felt my body melt and my fears fade as he held me in his arms. I felt his broken pride healing and the guilt dissipate. My throat burned, but I needed this kiss. I needed his warmth and comfort. Most of all, I needed to feel the love we shared.

"Candice, we shouldn't be doing this," Jax whispered, as he pulled away breathless.

"Why not?" I glared at him, as my voice came out breathy and hoarse.

"I don't think my boss wants to watch a porn." Jax indicated a man in a suit. I remembered him from Chase's funeral, and from the break-in at my house. He had been standing at the grave site where he'd spoken about a policeman's character. I remembered he had stayed beside Christina at the hospital when they told us of Chase's fate, and was beside her on the side of my house at the break-in as well. If I wasn't mistaken, he was the same man from the bar my first night in town.

The more I thought about all the events that took place, the more things slid together. All the lunches between Chase and Christina. The man in the suit who held her hand when I had lost him. The way Michelle clung to her at the funeral. Was I the only one, other than Jax, who didn't see it? Had I been blind?

How clueless could I have been if I didn't see what is so obvious now? I clung to Jax wondering if I was looking at him through rose-colored glasses as well. Maybe it was just the trauma from what Andrew had done, but things were coming into focus differently.

"I'm tired." I pulled myself off Jax. He shook hands with the man in the suit and they spoke a few words, seeming animated in their discussion. Then Jax walked over to Mark and Brooklyn who seemed to be staring at me with that *poor girl* look on her face. As Jax came back toward me, Mark and Brooklyn followed.

"Come on, Candy, let's get you settled," Jax stated, as we all filed out the door.

"My things?" I asked, and Jax turned around and grabbed my laptop and brought it out with us.

"This is all you need until they are done," he whispered as we headed down the hallway. I was making a mental note to always carry an extra bag because whenever the police came, they invaded my things and kept it with them until they were done.

Looking back, the police were all over my room and Andrew's room. When we got to the end of the hallway, there was a room with an open door that we walked inside.

Upon entry, there were people with guns and video cameras. It seemed they had cleared out the area to run surveillance. It was like something out of a movie. A short man began handing each of us bulletproof vests, and that was the moment I crumbled. I had sucked it up and stood tall while people came in and out of my hotel room. I had pretended I wasn't affected whenever Jax looked at me, but watching him put on a bulletproof vest broke everything inside me.

The moment of realization that I might die. The moment I realized the last face I made at my dad was one of anger as I stormed out of the restaurant.

"Candice, put it on. It is only a precaution while we move you to a new hotel," Brooklyn urged behind me.

I walked behind a screen. I wanted to drop to the floor and cry, but my heart wouldn't let me put more on Jax than he already had to deal with. My body trembled from the new stress of Jax being a target and someone wanting to hurt others just to get to him.

Jax walked behind my curtain and gave me a smile that didn't reach his eyes, as he attached the Velcro on my vest. I stared at his face as he made sure I was fastened in. When he finally did meet my eyes, it spoke volumes of worry and love. I could see that he was as scared for me as I was for him.

"Where are we going?" I whispered.

"Mark and I have some things we need to get from my house. Then we will move you to a safe house."

"You're coming too, right?" I asked, but the look on his face said the answer was no. He didn't say a word and he didn't have to. I knew he was going after Andrew, but it felt more like he was contemplating suicide.

"Won't he know to look for you at your house?"

"No. The house is covered. Vanessa knows that Mark and I play racquetball at nine in the morning every other day. We will go to my house at nine while Andrew is looking for me to play racquetball. We have other officers who will be at the courts, waiting to see if he shows. We have it covered. Don't worry."

My anger superseded my fear and reached a boiling point with the words *don't worry* coming out of Jax's mouth. Doing things his way was going to get him killed.

"Why don't I just call him and set up a meeting? He sent out notes for other officers to bring you to meet him, anyway. You have a price on your life. Let me call him and set up a place to meet. Then you can kill him when he comes." The entire room went silent. Officers began backing out of the room as if I had done something wrong.

The man with the salt and pepper hair in the suit walked up to me and took my hand in his. I wanted to take it back, but felt like that would convey the wrong message.

"Ms. Carson, I am Commissioner Donnelly. I believe we met at Detective Matson's funeral. I just want to tell you that I have the utmost faith in my detectives and their plan. I have been doing this a long time and would never allow them to be vigilantes. Our plan is to arrest Andrew Thomas and bring him in alive."

I did pull my hand back as I put my blue, off the shoulder sweater over the vest while I thought about it. This was not going to work. Chase went with one of their plans and got slaughtered. My body began to shiver with anxiety.

"I have something I need to do," I stated, as I grabbed my purse. Jax went to reach for my elbow and I gave him an evil smile that said *don't try to stop me.* I got out the door when Brooklyn came running up behind me.

"Where are we going?" she asked with a smile on her face.

"I am going to handle something. Where are you going?" I asked, as the elevator opened.

"I am going where you are going."

"Brooklyn, I might be committing a crime and you are the acting Assistant District Attorney. So you see where that could be a problem?"

"No, a lawyer is a lawyer. Besides, we work better when we have all the facts. What could be better than a bird's-eye view of the events?"

"Candice, wait!" Jax bellowed, but I nodded my head for Brooklyn to enter the elevator and walked in behind her.

"I have to do this, Jax." The elevator doors shut with a hurt look on his face. The face that said he thought this would be the last time we saw each other.

I thought about the characters in my books at that moment. I asked myself what they would do to achieve a happy ending and I drew a blank. If this was a book I had been writing, I would have written myself into a corner with no clue where to go.

I walked out to the street and headed west. Still working on the chain of events in my head, I wasn't certain where I was headed. Brooklyn caught my arm and held me there as she hailed a cab.

"Figured out what you are going to do yet?" she asked as we climbed into the cab. I had to buy some time.

"Take us to the Crossfit on Columbus Avenue," I shouted to the driver, finding my voice.

Brooklyn merely smiled at me. I didn't know how this was going to work. Anything illegal I did, my accomplice will also be my prosecutor.

"Brooklyn, we don't know each other very well. If you are not prepared to go the distance with whatever I do, I think you should jump ship now."

"Don't worry. I have our bail money."

Brooklyn reached across the cab and placed her hand on mine in a comforting way.

"Candice, I have been in your shoes before. I have wanted to save the people I loved by sacrificing myself. I know how you feel. I don't know what you have planned, but whatever it is, I'm in. Let's finish this, so our men won't have targets on their backs."

Chapter Seventeen

We sat in the cab outside the Crossfit while I thought about what to do next. The sun brightened as snow stopped falling. That meant I was on my own, no water nearby to wish on. No traffic jams to buy me time. It was do or die.

Vanessa emerged from the Crossfit and climbed into a maroon Honda.

"Follow that car," I shrieked, grabbing my throat from the pain. I don't even know why I shouted, just seemed like the thing to do. Brooklyn reached into her purse and held up two bottles. One was Tylenol and one was Motrin. I stared at her.

"I need you to be one hundred percent here. Pick your poison and let's get on with this!"

I was starting to like Brooklyn more and more. I already knew she and Mark had a thing going on. They tried not to let it show, but there was something dark and delicious going on between them. If whatever we did ended well, those two would wind up characters in my next book.

We followed Vanessa to her house and waited while she was inside. I would have done something there, but my writer's brain was coming up with all kinds of unrealistic situations that would not help. I needed a sign or something that said I was supposed to do this.

I never questioned my love for Jax. After the shock had worn off from Chase's death, I realized how much I loved Jax. The question was, did I love him enough to go to prison for life? Did I love him enough to put myself between him and Andrew? Did I love him enough to die for him?

"You have that look," Brooklyn stated.

"What look is that?" I stared out the window so my face would stay hidden and give nothing away.

"That look someone gets when they are trying to decide if they want justice served or if they want to become a vigilante."

"I was wondering if I loved him enough to die for him." I looked at Brooklyn, wishing she had answers, but I knew only I could answer that.

"Do you love him?" she asked, and I nodded. "Can you envision your life without him?" I shook my head. "It's simple. If you don't want to live without him, but one of you has to die, then you've already answered it. I would give up my life to save Mark, and he would do the same for me. Ask yourself this: would he die for you?"

As I stared down at my ring and it flickered in the sunlight, I knew what the answers were. I looked up in time to see a cab picking up Vanessa. I took a deep breath as we followed her to Trader Joe's.

I watched from a distance as Vanessa walked into Trader Joe's, and a thought came to me. Brooklyn nodded. I knew what we needed to do.

Next, Vanessa had the driver drop her off at Jax's house. She let herself in with the same spare key I had used. I wanted to rip every blonde hair out of her head at that moment. I seriously had to get my jealousy under control. I closed my eyes and took some deep breaths and tried to remember that she did not have a clue about what her brother had done, or how it dragged her into this.

We watched from outside the house as she put groceries away. I seriously felt like a stalker and was behaving like one as I watched her through the front window. I guess Andrew hadn't told her about me and Jax, or maybe she didn't care. Either way I was going to have to confront her and she would find out if she didn't already know.

"Are you sure this is what you want to do?" Brooklyn asked, making sure I was ready.

"Yes. Just be near the back door so when I unlock it you can come in."

"Here, take my scarf." Brooklyn handed me her blue scarf to cover the bruises on my neck that were still purpling under the skin.

Then I got out of the cab and headed for the front door. I walked up the steps and took a deep breath as I got close to the door. The last time I was here, Jax told me goodbye. It had cut me in a way I could never imagine. I wasn't going to feel that way again.

I rang the doorbell and waited. A few minutes passed by and I rang the doorbell again. Vanessa finally opened the door and stood before me in a black crop top sweater, a pair of skinny jeans with cut-outs everywhere and a pair of knee high biker boots.

I stared at her green eyes that looked nothing like Andrew's. I could not seem to find any family resemblance between the two. Maybe they were step-siblings because she was taller, leaner, and nothing matched up. If I didn't have to hate her, I would probably admit she was gorgeous.

"Yes, can I help you?" Vanessa asked, as if she didn't know who I was.

"I'm Candice, I was here the other day to see Jax."

"Oh, yes. I remember. What can I do for you?" Vanessa asked.

"I think I left my phone in the guest room when I was getting my luggage from Jax the other night. Can you see if it's up there?"

It was not the most creative lie I could have come up with, but it worked in the ten seconds it took me to create it.

"Sure. It's really cold out there, do you want to come inside while I go look?" Vanessa asked sweetly, opening the door for me to enter. She was being so polite I almost felt guilty about what was going to happen here. I almost felt bad that she was related to the lunatic who left me covering my neck with a scarf.

"Yes, thank you," I replied and walked inside.

When Vanessa headed up the stairs, I ran to the back door and unlocked it. Brooklyn came in and immediately went into the pantry in the kitchen to act as either a witness or my shooter, considering her holster was popped and she was ready.

"I am winging this, so just go with it," I whispered to Brooklyn as we cracked the door. Then I ran for the couch and sat down, waiting for Vanessa to return.

When Vanessa started down the stairs, my phone rang. I closed my eyes as I reached into my purse and pulled it out. I was already busted, so I might as well answer it.

"Hello."

"Where the hell are you?" Jax asked.

"Your house," I replied, and Vanessa eyed me eerily.

"I am coming to get you, do not move." He spoke in a determined tone. It was the alpha in him that he used at work.

"I love you." I spoke softly and hung up.

Vanessa walked down the stairs and placed her hands on her hips. I still could not find any family resemblance. The look on her face said that the truth was going to come out faster than I had planned. I thought it would take more than a few minutes before I would have to spill my guts to her.

"Was that *my Jax* on your phone?" Vanessa asked with disdain dripping off her words.

"Yes, sorry! I must have had my phone all along. I have been so forgetful with being back in town with jetlag and everything." I was lying as fast as I could, but they were horrid lies that anyone could have seen through.

"Is that his mother's ring you're wearing?" Vanessa asked, and I noticed I had it out on display with the way I held the phone.

"I guess this is the moment I tell you we need to talk," I whispered.

I expected violence and shouting, but Vanessa merely sat on the recliner next to the couch. She waited patiently, as I had months before, when Christina was sitting in the same seat. I knew what she was feeling because I was feeling the same betrayal that night as well. For a split second, I felt bad about being the other woman.

"Is Jax going to leave me?" Vanessa asked. The look on her face said she was preparing to hear the worst. My heart ached with pain for what I was about to say. I didn't want anyone hurt, I didn't want any of us in this situation, but I hadn't put us here. I was merely trying to fix it so everyone could go on with their lives.

"I could tell you yes out of some jealous need to hurt you, but I would be lying. He told me he wasn't leaving you, but that he wanted me to wait for him."

I watched as her cheeks flamed on her pale skin, and the same rosy color formed around her eyes as tears formed.

"Are you sleeping with him?" she asked, and I was actually shocked she was taking this as well as she was. When I had been told there was another woman, I wanted to claw her face off. I guess that made Vanessa a better woman than me.

"Does it matter?" I asked softly.

"No, I guess it doesn't. What did I do wrong?" Vanessa asked. Now I was seriously concerned, because she was taking this extremely well. Not to mention how could you forget that your brother is a psycho who wants to kill your boyfriend. I guess this was the moment I was about to ask.

"Vanessa, what did you expect? Your brother killed my fiancé. Jax was never going to let that go. Even if he had let it go, your brother is coming for Jax."

Vanessa wiped the tears from her cheeks and looked at me with confusion in her eyes.

"I don't have a brother." Her voice had turned brittle as she held back unshed tears.

"Yes, you do. They were able to link you back to him. Jax has known all along. He wanted to get close to you to kill your brother for killing his partner."

Vanessa stood up and began pacing in front of the fireplace. She went back and forth as her hands went to her hips, then she crossed them and repeated this as she continued to pace. Finally, she turned and looked at me as if I was the enemy. In a way, I guess I was.

"I do not have a brother. I have an ex-husband who is Alejandro Torres. He is sometimes called Andrew Thomas. He has a brother named Niko."

I hadn't seen that coming and I am a writer. Brooklyn apparently didn't either, because she emerged from the pantry looking like she had just eaten a bug. Then her face changed and she began making phone calls.

"Andrew is your ex-husband?" I murmured.

I stood up from the couch and walked over to the window. There was a storm moving in, but for once it wasn't pleasant. I felt like this was goodbye. We didn't know anything we thought we had. The information collected had been false and Jax was headed here. I took off my jacket and scarf and dumped them on the couch. I pulled my hair behind my shoulders in a nervous habit and turned to look at Brooklyn, who was obviously talking to Mark.

"Tell them not to come here," I shouted hoarsely at her.

"What the hell is going on? And what is wrong with your neck?" Vanessa asked.

"My neck was compliments of your ex-husband. He is coming to kill Jax. He is the one who killed my fiancé."

Vanessa seemed to take her anger down a notch and walked into the kitchen. She pulled out a bottle of whiskey and set it down. Then she poured three shots. "Well, if we are going to die today, I am going out with no pain," she said.

"Why would we die today?" Brooklyn asked, as she put away her phone.

"Andrew gets rid of anything in his way. If we're in the way of him getting to Jax, then we are all dead." Vanessa took a shot. Her hands shook and her face displayed the fear she felt whenever she spoke of Andrew.

Moments like these made me think I might be in an alternate universe. Andrew had been so nice and caring. He made me breakfast every morning and helped me get noticed at work after my first boss died and he took over. I guess when people always complained their bosses were dicks, they weren't kidding, because Andrew was acting like a homicidal asshole.

My writer's brain was still trying to develop why he would have gotten close to me. I had cut Jax out of my life. I didn't share many personal details with him until he told me about the trip to New York.

"I am not going to let him kill Jax," I shouted, even though it pained my throat. "I am not going to let anyone else die."

Brooklyn and I walked over to the couch and sat down. She opened iCloud on her phone and began scrolling through the files her office had transferred to her. We both looked to see what was missed and where someone had gone wrong. There had to be something there. I would never accept this man I'd known for months had murdered Chase and planned to murder Jax and there was nothing I could do about it.

There were hundreds of photos of Vanessa with Andrew, but in every photo his face had been obscured, as if he'd known where the surveillance was. It must have dawned on us both at the same time that he had someone on the inside.

Brooklyn and I exchanged a glance as it became clear this was higher than drug dealing. No record existed of Chase arresting him, which made it more of a mystery. *Why would he kill Chase?*

I ran upstairs to Jax's room and pulled out the key that was taped to the top of his drawer in the nightstand. I then opened the gun safe.

"What are you doing?" Brooklyn asked, as Vanessa came to a halt in the doorway beside her. They both stared at me as if I had finally lost my mind, and maybe I had, but if I was going to lose my life tonight, I would be armed and ready to battle.

"If he has someone on the inside, then he would know Mark and Jax are headed here. Call them back and tell them to go radio silent."

"How do you know that?" Vanessa asked.

"If this were a story I had written, it would be the next step. It just makes sense for the next plausible step to be Andrew going to where Jax was headed and killing him."

I started loading guns, thankful that Chase and Jax had made me go to the range for them to learn how to shoot and take care of a weapon. I began with the AR-15 that Jax had gotten right before Chase had died. From the looks of it, he had not even cleaned it. They had both gotten one to take to the shooting range days before Chase had died.

Then I moved on to the twelve-gauge and the four nine millimeter handguns. I was grateful Jax liked to spend his paychecks stocking up on ammunition. We had enough here to go to war and that's exactly where we were headed.

Brooklyn called Mark and explained what I had said. I heard a lot of complaining coming through the phone, but Brooklyn knew how to talk to Mark to get them to agree. I actually smiled when I heard her talking to him. No matter what he seemed to say, she was able to curve it so the conversation went her way. *She must be one hell of a prosecutor.*

I didn't know where the guys were going to be, but my head was telling me if this were a great story, they would be somewhere nearby, which made me nervous for their safety. I put two guns in the waistband of my jeans and handed one each to Brooklyn and Vanessa.

"You ever fired a weapon before?" I asked Vanessa. It was a given that Brooklyn knew how to handle a gun, since she wore one on her body.

I passed out the rifles and I kept the shotgun as Vanessa shook her head. Brooklyn began explaining how to check to make sure the safety was off, and where to look down the sights. We briefed Vanessa quickly but the whiskey bottle in her hand said she wasn't retaining anything we said.

Brooklyn and Vanessa headed downstairs as a noise drew me into the guest room. I opened the door to see the window was open and the rain was pooling on the floor. Even in my anxiousness, my brain reminded me of better moments like that first night with Jax when rain pooled on the floor and even splashed on his lip. As if an angel had dropped it there to entice me after I had had my heart broken.

I shook the thoughts from my mind and forced myself to go downstairs. I placed the shotgun beside the recliner on the side, so it wouldn't be visible but it remained close to me. I sat down where I'd once talked to Christina, and I waited for Andrew to come.

Within a half hour there was a knock on the door. I leaned back in the recliner. Vanessa ran to the pantry like a coward. Brooklyn went to the door and opened it with her hand on the grip of the gun in the back of her pants.

Once again, a knock on the door held something unexpected. I was going to have lingering issues about people knocking if every time someone knocked it wasn't what I expected.

"Christina, what are you doing here?" Brooklyn asked, as she opened the door and Christina walked in.

"I wanted to make sure Candice was all right." Then she turned to look at me.

It was at that moment everything became clear. Her green eyes were the same as Andrew's. Her lightly tanned skin was just a shade or two lighter than Andrew's. The red hair threw me, but she naturally had dark brown hair. They even walked the same and talked the same.

Brooklyn let go of the door and the wind from the storm slammed it shut as the gusts carried through the house. Christina stared at me and knew that I knew. I placed my hand on my gun and waited.

"You love Jax?" I asked, and she glared at me.

"I did, until you ruined what we could have had."

"You slept with my fiancé and had his baby. You think you could have had something with Jax, and now you have a psycho brother coming after him. What the fuck do you think I did?" Rage flooded my veins.

I could be accused of being a coward for running away. I could be accused of being the other woman for sleeping with a taken man. I could even be accused of being gullible enough not to have seen this coming from the beginning. I couldn't wait to hear what else I was being accused of.

"Your letter." Christina gritted her teeth, placing her hands on her hips. Brooklyn moved to the kitchen and pulled Vanessa out of the pantry. They sat at the island and watched as the invisible daggers were thrown between Christina and me.

"What letter?" I asked, standing up and stepping around the coffee table. Christina reached into her pocket and unfolded an envelope with a pink note inside. I suddenly realized what she meant, but we were already circling the couch.

"Dear Jax." Christina started reading the letter out loud. I lunged for it, but she moved away from me. Then we began circling each other as if we were animals in a pen and only the strongest would survive.

"Dear Jax, I didn't want to do this. I didn't want to run away without a goodbye. You gave me something I can never thank you for. You made me feel good when I felt my worst. You gave me the good to go with the bad. I have strong feelings for you that became evident when I let you inside me. I am not strong enough to replace Chase and stay here with you. There are memories of Chase everywhere I look and am just not ready to have anyone replace the role he played in my life. I loved him with all my heart and soul, and the way I feel right now, I love you with all my heart and soul as well."

"Here comes my favorite part," Christina said, moving in front of the fireplace. I wanted to grab the guns in the back of my jeans and shoot her in the face, but I wouldn't.

"When the clouds roll in and sing you a thunderous song, please know that glorious event is the world's way of telling you I am thinking of you. I will love you with every breath I take until I take my last. I will always and forever be your water-wishing girl."

I watched as Christina crumpled the letter and tossed it into the fireplace. She flipped the switch on the wall and turned it on. I watched my words burn, and turn to ash. She was lucky she hadn't reached for the fireplace remote on the coffee table, because I probably would have punched her.

"I took it from his nightstand so he would stop reading your lies. I thought he would grow to hate you. It helped when he went to California and you were happy after Andrew took over as your boss. All Andrew had to do was play Jax's part and you were happy. Jax saw and came home, and removed you from his heart."

"What are you doing here, Christina?" I asked, as I reached for her and she moved farther away.

"Brooklyn, we should make popcorn," Vanessa called out, proving she'd had one shot too many. Brooklyn shushed her and I lunged for Christina while her head was turned.

I pulled her to the ground and climbed on top of her. I punched her in the face as she reached up and tried to restrain my hands. Then she flipped us and she was on top of me. I didn't care. I reached up and ripped her hair out as she slapped me. Then I punched her in the face with all the force I could gather, and the blow was so strong I managed to knock two of her teeth out. I had to shake my hand, it hurt so bad. Then we rolled again so I was on top. I continued to punch her while I screamed at her.

"You let them kill Chase. You were going to let them kill Jax. Now I am going to kill you, bitch!"

Chapter   Eighteen

Christina and I were fighting on the floor between the fireplace and coffee table. Blood was dripping from my mouth down onto her as her blood pooled on the hardwood floor from the two missing teeth and the scratches I had given her. I would surely wear a black eye as she would sport a broken nose.

She punched upward and hit my chin. I retaliated, punching her in the ribs, and smirked as she gasped. I had knocked the air out of her and it felt good. I have never in my life wanted to kill anyone more than I wanted to kill her. I was so into the moment that I didn't hear anyone say my name. I was focused on hurting her until I felt hands pick me up and I began swinging on whoever had me.

"Candice, stop." I heard Jax's voice and felt arms hold me down. I reached behind me and placed a hand on my gun just as I realized who it was. My adrenaline was coursing through me and I was having trouble gaining control of my body to keep the tremors down.

Jax carried me over to the couch and sat down, placing me in his lap. He had a tight grip on me, so there was very little I could do. I watched as Vanessa ate the popcorn she apparently had made for the fight. Brooklyn and Mark hugged, while Christina laid on the floor groaning.

"You know I can arrest you," Jax whispered in my ear.

"Do it! The punishment would be worth the crime," I bellowed.

Jax held me tight as I struggled to come down from the high.

"Brooklyn, why didn't you break up the fight?" Jax asked as I slowed my breathing down. Looking down at Christina lying on the floor bleeding soothed an ache I'd had in me for months.

"I felt like Candice had it under control."

Mark hugged her to him and I relished the relationship they had. I slowed my anger down and laid back on Jax. Christina started to get up and I kicked my leg at her to make her lay back down.

"I will handcuff you and put you in the car if you cannot restrain yourself."

"Handcuffs might be kinky," I responded with a light kiss on the lips. I winced slightly. My lips were sore and swollen from getting hit. Jax smiled at me and loosened his hold as I calmed down.

"You went from beating someone up to being flirty. I swear, you women are like rollercoasters. I never know which way you're going to go next."

Brooklyn and Mark laughed at the comment as thunder shook the house. I felt a draft roll through as the storm strengthened. I looked out the kitchen window and swore I saw Chase looking at me with disappointment. I closed my eyes and opened them again and there was nothing there but a branch scraping the window.

I would now wonder if my behavior was the wrong thing to do. I would love to say it was the right thing to do because it felt right, but that was not always true. I had been wanting to mangle Christina's face for months, but now I had guilt settled in my veins.

Jax sat me down on the couch and glared at me as if to say *don't move*. Then he walked over to the freezer and retrieved a bag of frozen peas.

"You should eat fresh organic veggies," I stated as he came near.

"You should learn not to fight unless it's in Jell-O," Jax retorted, and laughter was heard throughout the room.

"I love you, Jax." I whispered, as Jax sat on the couch beside me.

"I absolutely adore you. You make me want to be a better man."

He placed the cold peas over my eyes as the storm knocked out the power. Jax used his cell phone to light up the way to the kitchen, where he pulled out candles and began lighting them all over the house.

"Jax, you shouldn't be here," I whispered, as he came closer. He mumbled something, but I couldn't hear it over Christina's persistent groaning. I watched Vanessa pick up the popcorn and bring it to the coffee table. She set it down and placed her hands in her back pockets and stared at Jax.

"I guess it's over?" Vanessa said in a saddened tone to Jax. I hate that she got hurt over nothing. Christina and Andrew had planned this entire charade and it hurt a lot of people. I hope they went to jail for a long time.

"I'm sorry. I wish I could say it's not. But the truth is, Candice owns that part of me you want. You are a wonderful woman and deserve better than what I have given you over the last few months."

"These last few months were everything I needed," Vanessa whispered as she looked away from him.

It was hard to watch him break her heart. I wondered if that was what I looked like when Chase died. Vanessa took a candle and excused herself to go upstairs into the guest room. There was no leaving with the storm raging on as it was, and it had to be hard on her to stay here with us.

"What's with all my guns being out?" Jax asked, as he turned to look at me.

"I am prepared for war," I replied.

"Who are you going to war with?"

"Andrew."

Everyone quieted. No one had anything else to say, apparently. I heard sobs coming from upstairs. I excused myself as thunder rumbled loudly through the house. I walked up and knocked on the door, but Vanessa didn't answer.

I turned the doorknob and walked in. It was dark and the only light came from the candle in the bathroom.

"Vanessa, are you all right?" I asked, creeping into the room.

Suddenly, there were hands over my mouth, applying pressure over my busted lip. I heard scuffling around and averted my eyes to see that Brent was holding Vanessa.

"Miss me, Candy?" Andrew whispered in my ear, and a shiver traveled down my spine.

I tried to elbow his chest and kick behind me to get him to let me go. I struggled and fought, but he was so much stronger than I was at the moment. I had exhausted most of my energy on his sister. I hoped someone would hear, but the thunder grew louder as the storm descended.

"I love it when you fight me. It makes killing you so much more enjoyable. Fight me, Candy. Fight me harder," Andrew muttered.

I found renewed strength and began fighting him again. I tried to get my gun from the back of my jeans, but he had me too tight. When I heard the thunder settle I wanted to scream for help, but there was no way I was going to let him use me as bait to get to Jax.

As the thunder rumbled again, we fought and moved around the room as I aimed to get us over to the window. It was still open and water had pooled on the floor. Vanessa allowed herself to be subdued and stopped fighting Brent. There was defeat written across her face.

As we moved closer to the window, I used a maneuver I learned in the self-defense class Chase had made me take. I stepped on his foot as hard as I could and elbowed him in the gut. When he leaned forward, I threw my hand back to hit him in the nose. The second I got some distance between us, I kicked him in the groin and reached for my weapon. The weapon wasn't there.

"Looking for this?" Brent asked, from where he held Vanessa right behind me.

"Let her go." I pleaded with Brent while Andrew groaned, cupping what was left of his manhood. Lightning cracked and the storm raged over the house.

"No, she belongs to us. She ran away from Andrew which is why we are here. Right, Niko?"

A man walked out of the bathroom. He was short and stocky. He didn't look like anyone Andrew could be related to.

"Vanessa should never have run from us. We came here to find her and your police detectives stumbled across a shipment of women. Let's just say the first dead cop was a warning," Niko uttered, as I watched him lean on the door frame.

Questions raced through my mind. What if I screamed? What if I ran? What if I did nothing?

"You bitch!" Andrew groaned, as he stood up and backhanded me. It sent me to the window as I struggled to catch myself before tumbling out. I was going to fall.

Andrew came at me and I stopped trying to catch myself and fell out of the window. I landed on Jax's shrubs. I felt as though every bone in my body had been hit with a sledgehammer. The impact made me think I was dying, but the cold heavy rain cascading down my face wouldn't let me give up.

I rolled off the bush and crawled to the back door as the rain turned to hail. I was so battered and bruised I couldn't stand up. I knocked on the door and waited. No one could hear me with the storm raging on. I slapped the door until Brooklyn finally opened it and yelled for Mark and Jax.

Jax lunged for me. He helped me to my feet and carried me to the couch to look me over.

"What happened?" Jax asked, as he pushed my wet hair off my face. I merely pointed and took a second to get the energy to speak.

"Andrew is in the guest room," I whispered in agony.

Just then, gunshots rang out in the guest room. I nearly fainted with the thought that Vanessa was dead. I didn't know her well, but I knew she was innocent. She did not deserve this.

Jax and Mark pulled their weapons and headed up the stairs. Jax went into his room to come through the bathroom while Mark busted through the guest room door.

The five minutes I laid on the couch waiting with Brooklyn by my side for more gunshots seemed like an eternity. Seconds ticked by as slowly as centuries. I saw Mark first as he came down the stairs, his gun holstered. He walked over to Brooklyn and whispered something that had her reaching for her phone. Then he reached for his phone.

I turned my attention back to the stairs and saw Jax carrying Vanessa down the stairs as she trembled and cried. When he sat her on the recliner, she had blood splattered all over her.

Within a half hour, the house was swarming with people coming and going. The rains had finally subsided when the coroner rolled out Andrew, Niko, and Brent. There were medics looking over Vanessa and myself. They had to call out a separate ambulance for Christina, and I pleaded with them to leave her to suffer the injustice of not being a priority.

"How are you?" Brooklyn asked from behind me.

"Sore, but I will live. Thanks for coming with me. This is not what I expected, but I am grateful you were here."

"Anytime." Brooklyn leaned in, whispering, "I still have your bail money if you need it."

I laughed, then cringed because it hurt my body. Jax gave me a telling look that said he was worried about me. I offered a light nod to tell him I was okay, and focused my attention back to Brooklyn.

"How is Vanessa?" I asked in a whisper.

"She is in shock. She claims a man appeared out of nowhere and killed the three of them and then disappeared just as quickly."

"Is that what happened?" I asked, perplexed.

"In my experience, the victims choose how they remember things because it is easier for them to digest their role in it. She also might think she would be charged with their deaths if she is not familiar with the court system."

"In my eyes, she's a hero," I murmured as I watched them getting ready to take Vanessa to be evaluated.

"In my eyes, *you* are the hero." Brooklyn nudged my shoulder with hers.

"Come again?" I asked.

"Candice, you came back to a place you feared. You stepped up and accepted responsibility for your actions. You let go of Chase and Jax. That alone took courage, but then you forgave those who had said or done things to hurt you, like Jax and Christina. Then you became a justice-delivering badass. You, my new friend, are my hero."

Brooklyn walked off to handle the political side of this mess as the commissioner arrived. I watched as the commissioner's expression turned to anger as Brooklyn explained what had happened.

Not long after, he had Christina handcuffed. With the press outside to get the photo-op, he took her arm and began to walk her out. I made myself scarce, but followed.

Then I overheard the commissioner whisper something. "Don't worry, sweetheart. I will have you fixed up and back home by dinner." No one else had heard.

"Excuse me," I called out as they reached the car. "I heard what you said. Why would she get to go home by dinner?"

"It's none of your business." The commissioner spoke quietly, but kept his smile for the cameras. I grabbed his arm and jerked it toward me.

"Get your hands off my husband!" Christina seethed, and shock reverberated through me. I dropped his arm and stepped back. Everything else in the world ceased to exist at that moment. It was just them versus me.

"Your husband?" I asked, with a need to hear it again. "You ordered Chase's murder, and you put Andrew in my life. You altered the files and told Andrew where the police would be." I covered my mouth as I watched his eyes glimmer and a smirk slide across his face.

"They intervened in an effort to make me more money than the city of New York ever gave me. Sorry for your loss, but Chase should have stayed out of it. Now, walk away, princess, or Mark and Jax will be running for the rest of their lives."

"You son of a bitch!" I shouted, slamming my fist into the commissioner's face. I felt the pain immediately and pulled my hand down. I shook it as Brooklyn and Mark ran for me.

I lunged for the commissioner, but found strong hands around my waist. I looked like some psycho as the news cameras turned on me. I quickly calmed down and composed myself.

"What the hell?" Brooklyn said. "I can only keep you out of so much trouble. I can't help you with this."

"Why did you just assault the commissioner?" Mark asked.

"He ordered Chase's murder. Christina is his wife."

"What evidence do you have?" Mark asked.

"I heard him!" I exclaimed in a panic, because I had no hard proof. My heart raced and sweat broke out across my face. Jax stood on the porch and looked at me as though I had hurt him. Then a woman walked up to Mark and Brooklyn.

"Sir, my name is Kelly McDaniel, a reporter for News Channel Five. I have the proof. Our sound truck was able to pick up the entire conversation."

Chapter Nineteen

The days came and went quickly as my body healed, and the commissioner pled guilty in exchange for a lighter sentence. He had to give up his operation, but since no one could trust him, the FBI was being called in to verify the operation had been shut down.

My dad and Michelle started dating and I was happy for them, even if I thought it was a little bit weird. I can't say I didn't see it coming, as they had been spending every day together. They were even taking care of Chelle as if she was their own child.

Michelle had filed papers to start the process to adopt Chelle. It was only natural since Chase was dead and Christina should never be allowed to leave prison. I knew my dad and Michelle would do whatever was necessary to make sure Chelle was raised right. They did, after all, raise me in their own ways. I might be a little jealous, but I carried a mean right hook and an open heart. All in all, I would say they did a great job with me, and they would do the same for Chelle.

I sat at The Cafeteria and waited for my dad to come and eat with me. We had made weekly dates together, and we were finally getting to know each other again. I had an understanding of how he felt when my mom died and he began to see me as more than just a child who looked like the woman he had lost.

"Hi, Candy Cane," my dad called out, then placed a kiss on the top of my head.

"Hi, Dad. How are you?"

"I am great! Have you decided to move back here and put the house in California up for sale yet?" He spoke with a detective's demeanor, having spent too much time with Jax and Mark. Some of their habits should have stayed with them.

"Dad, I have someone renting it on a month-to-month basis until I decide what to do with it."

He smiled at me as the waitress came and took our orders. We both got the banana split waffles. Something we had been eating together since I was a little girl.

"I have something I want to talk to you about, Candy."

"Dad, is this one of those conversations where I get mad, then you get mad, then we avoid each other for a week?" I asked, because his words sounded an awful lot like *we need to talk,* and that never ends well.

"I don't think so, Candy." He looked at me with confusion on his face.

"Then let's hear it, Dad. What's up?"

He paused for a long moment, as if choosing his words carefully before voicing them. This made me nervous. I didn't know what to expect.

"Candy, you are my only daughter, so your opinion is very important to me."

My dad started talking and I gripped the napkin into a ball and squeezed. I thought it would soften the blow of whatever he was trying to say.

"What happened to you scared me. It made me take a serious look at our relationship and my life. I push for these meals together so we can have some time together. After all, I am not getting any younger."

I gasped quietly as I thought about a time in which my dad would no longer be with me. I couldn't imagine it because I had just gotten him back. What was he about to say? Where was he going with this conversation?

"Candy, I love you and Jax. You are both my children. I will always remember Chase, but I think it is time you moved on. I should, too. I should have let your mom go, and allowed her to rest in peace knowing we were happy, but I couldn't. I see you doing the same thing I did, and it is a life of loneliness."

Tears began to fill my eyes. I had been trying to let go for a while, but something out there kept me holding on. Something out there told me Chase and I were not done yet. Jax told me he felt the same way, that it was part of healing.

The first stage of grieving is denial. I was stuck there. I had floated into anger, but then quickly went back to denial. I would always strive to get through the five stages, wondering if I would ever get my heart back.

"Candy, did you hear me?" Dad squeezed my hand across the table. I shook my thoughts and smiled for him.

"Sorry, Dad. What did you say?"

"I want to ask Michelle to move in with me. I need to know how you feel about it."

"Isn't that a little fast?" I asked, concern invading my thoughts.

"We both live alone. We are both going to help raise Chelle together. We want to sell our houses and move into a bigger place with room for us all."

I held my breath until my lungs hurt. Thinking of my dad with anyone other than my mom was painful. I had to remind myself that she was gone and he was here. She would want him to be happy.

"Are you two going to get married?" I asked, with reservations about where the conversation might lead. This was uncharted waters and I wasn't sure of what my reaction would be.

"No, Candy. We just want the companionship and we want to raise Chelle together. I will never be married to anyone but your mother, and Michelle feels the same way about Steven. We both lost our spouses, but that shouldn't stop us from having a companionship, or friendship, that allows us to help each other raise a baby."

For some reason that statement made me feel better. I took in my dad's appearance. He had a serene look about him, a happiness that had never been present before. I was happy he was moving on from my mom, but at the same time I didn't want anyone to forget her.

"Let's talk about you and Jax," he stated, pulling me out of my observations.

"What about us?" I asked quietly.

"Have you seen him since that day?"

"Not really."

"Why not?"

"I want to be with him, Dad, but he doesn't want me if I can't let go of Chase. I don't know why I keep holding on. Chase is gone and he is never coming back. I don't know how to accept that and put it behind me."

"Candy, I don't think you are giving much credit to Jax. I think you are the one keeping him away. He came to see me recently about you. I think the man will take you any way he can get you, even if that means he will have to share your heart with a dead man. You should really go see him."

My dad squeezed my hand and smiled at me as a tear fell from my eye. He was right. I had erected a wall around myself and wanted to keep everyone out. I didn't want to be hurt again. I also didn't want to hurt anyone else by my actions.

"All right, dad. I will go see him after we are done eating."

"I think you should go now. He is out at the river." Dad winked and nodded.

"But these are banana-split waffles." I whimpered like a child and stuck out my bottom lip.

"I think you will find that what is waiting for you is more important than your calorie splurge." Dad started to help me stand up. I turned to hug him and saw Michelle and Chelle coming to join him. That was the moment I realized my dad never wanted to have breakfast with me.

"Hi Michelle," I whispered over my dad's shoulder, and she grinned. Chelle reached her arms out for my dad as I let him go. She really was a doll-baby. I stood back and watched in awe as my dad took Chelle into his arms and hugged Michelle. They had taken a broken situation and made a family from it. I needed to find a way to do the same.

The cab pulled up outside of the banquet hall where the toasting farewell had been held. There were a ton of cars in the parking lot. They had loud music playing, letting me know I would have to sneak around back.

I walked around the building and followed the path into the woods alongside the river. I could have taken the cab to the lighthouse, but wanted a moment to prepare myself. My nerves kicked in as I knew this would be the first time I would be seeing Jax since it all went down. The man had been my best friend for years, but he still made my stomach flutter as if I had butterflies inside.

Vanessa still talked to him. I knew, because Brooklyn and I had become really good friends and she was nosy. I didn't have a clue why Vanessa stayed around.

It still amazed me how life could throw a curveball. I felt like it was throwing me one now. He might be about to tell me he wanted to stay with Vanessa. That could be why he chose our favorite place as kids to meet with me. He wanted to soften the blow by taking me to the water's edge where our names were carved in the tree near the run-down park where an old wishing well used to be.

As I approached the old trees, I saw jars with lightning bugs inside leading the way. The sun had set just enough to show me something was lit in the distance. My curiosity led me away from the water and toward the lights.

I edged forward and walked quietly as I investigated the source. I looked left and right as I didn't remember much of this area anymore. The rains had pushed the water up to the trees we played around as kids. As the sun set completely, I could see a brick-and-mortar wishing well lit up behind the trees where we had carved our names.

I came upon it and saw the gray bricks were freshly laid in the dirt, but the mortar mix had dried already. The roof was angled and shingled with charcoal. The posts holding up the roof had lighthouses carved into the wood and ivy wrapped around each side.

It was the most beautiful thing I had ever seen. I walked in a circle around it until I heard my steps grow louder and firmer. I looked down to see a stone walkway. I followed it around the tree where three little kids had carved their names one night in a pact to always stay together.

On the western side of the tree was a metal and wood couple's bench. When I got all the way around the tree I found Jax. He faced the water, deep in thought. I swallowed hard at the sweaty male in front of me.

"Jax?" I whispered. He slowly turned around and smiled at me. He looked at me as if I was the only woman in the world. My stomach fluttered and my pulse raced. "Jax, did you build me that wishing well?" I asked in a whisper. My mouth grew dry as he stepped closer.

"I did." Jax spoke in a silvery tone that had me wanting to run to him, mount him, taste him, or even just be near him.

"It's beautiful," I said softly. I waited for him to kiss me, hold me, or do something, but he merely stood there.

"Turn around."

I turned around to see street pole lamps and I walked up the slight incline to find our park had been completely repaired. I walked up to the green sign. I nearly cried when I read it. *The Chase Matson Park, dedicated to all those whose lives are taken too soon.*

I placed my hands over my face as tears swelled in my eyes. I pulled it together and turned and walked back to Jax. He looked so handsome and confident, but I hadn't forgotten Vanessa had been around.

As I came upon him, I wanted to scream at him to wrap his muscular arms around me. I felt torn between acting on impulse and waiting to hear what he was going to say. My brain wanted to scream at him to do something, and at the same time my heart said wait and find out why he had done all this.

"Why did you do this, Jax?" I whispered.

"I wanted to save the park. You were worried Chase would be forgotten, and that made me think about how his name could live on. This ensures that someone out there in the world will always know his name even if they didn't know him. This will be a place his daughter can come and play. This is the park that was saved because her father died."

"Why did you build the well and the bench?" I asked as I swallowed hard. Seeing the park look like new was a walk down memory lane I hadn't been prepared for. As if it had been healed while I still questioned when I would be. It gave me a renewed hope that everything could heal, even me.

Jax took my hand and led me in front of the bench. There, he turned me to face the old oak tree and placed my hand over the names carved into the bark. His hand covered mine as his fingers slid in between mine.

"We made a promise a long time ago to be together forever," Jax whispered in my ear. "I want my *wife* to be happy and have wonderful memories. I also wanted her to have a place to be able to make her wishes whenever she wants."

"Your wife?" I swallowed hard. This was the part where he dumped me. He had never asked me to marry him, and it was clear Vanessa had been around a lot lately. He had been with her long enough that they must've bonded. Maybe his time with me showed him what he would miss if she were gone.

"Yes, my wife." Jax pulled his hand down. I felt his body pull off mine as he backed away. I held my breath, tracing his name on the tree. I tried my best to guard my heart, but there was no protecting it from Jax because he owned it. I sucked up my pride and turned to him.

"When are you getting married?" I asked in a quiet rush.

"As soon as you say yes." Jax dropped to one knee, holding up a box which I assumed had another ring in it. I took the box and opened it. I gasped at the beautiful necklace inside.

It was a sterling silver lighthouse with a diamond in place of the light. My eyes filled with tears as I stood speechless. This was exactly what I wanted, and completely different compared to the *hey, you want to get married* speech Chase had given me.

"Yes!" I screamed as Jax started to put the necklace on me. It was only a matter of seconds after the clasp had locked that his hands were on my waist, and his lips on my neck. I no longer needed to wish in the wishing well. As he pulled my sweater off, I realized he was everything I needed. Everything I wanted. Everything I could ever hope for. Here and now, near a vacant park and a lighthouse that led ships home, it was my turn to make him scream my name.

Chapter Twenty

Over a year ago, I walked down the same streets from the church to the cemetery. I had climbed the same hill and stood before the same tree that I buried Chase under, and once more I came to say goodbye. A year ago, I didn't know how. I still didn't think I knew how, but I knew I had to try so that Jax and I could live a happy life together.

I stood before Chase's grave and took a shuddering breath as my eyes burned while I held back tears.

"I don't know why I am here. It is my wedding day and I am supposed to be the happiest woman in the world."

I spoke quietly even though I was in the cemetery alone. No one was around to cast judgment on me. No one to watch my insanity spill out while I pleaded with a dead man.

"Chase, I loved you. I will always love you, but since you are no longer here, I opened up what was left of my heart for Jax. I want to be with him. I want to love him, care for him, and be his wife. I came to ask you if I could have my heart back, so I can go into this marriage whole-heartedly."

Tears filled my eyes as I laid down beside Chase on the grass. I closed my eyes and waited for the storm on the edge of town to come in and drown my tears and set me free.

An hour passed and nothing had happened. No sign of Chase releasing me to Jax, no storm as it had dissipated and was not coming. Nervous, I took a deep breath as I sat up to discover Brooklyn standing at the bottom of the hill. She was waiting for me to take me to get dressed and then we were going to the water's edge to have our photos taken.

I waved down the hill at her and held up a finger, asking for one more minute. She nodded and rolled up the window.

"Chase, you may not want to give me a sign that you approve of this marriage. You may not want to give me my heart back, but I am going to get it back. I am going to be happy and you are going to live on inside my heart with Jax."

I put my fingers to my lips and kissed them. Then I moved my hand down to the tombstone and uttered those words once again. "Goodbye, Chase."

I walked slowly down the hill when a rumble of thunder sounded behind me. I turned around to see a small storm cloud had survived and was building. It looked as though this one little cloud would set off an enormous storm with tons of water drops to carry the wishes of others. As the storm strengthened, I realized it would surely rain on my wedding day and I couldn't be happier.

I finished descending the hill and headed to the church. I put on the dress I would only wear once, as Brooklyn slipped into a long black halter dress. We both grabbed our tuxedoed calla lily bouquets and smiled at each other. It was time to go.

"You have everything? Are you ready to go?" Brooklyn asked, as I started to open the door to the waiting car.

"Yeah, I think I am finally ready," I whispered to myself, as the first raindrop splattered on my forehead. Then I got into the car and we headed off to have wedding photos taken before the ceremony began.

We pulled up outside the lighthouse on Roosevelt Island. It wasn't our lighthouse, but this one was more accessible, and we needed a new place to create memories. This is where Jax had asked me to wait for him. This would be the place I told my kids about.

The photographer was there, but I didn't see Jax. I shook all the horrid thoughts away and climbed out of the car with Brooklyn, my maid of honor.

The sky churned in the distance to tell us the rain was holding off but not for long. It seemed we would have a limited window to get the photos done before we all got drenched.

Brooklyn and I took our photos together. It wasn't long before Mark showed up in his tuxedo, looking extra yummy for Brooklyn. She eyed him as if he was an *all you can eat*, calorie-free buffet.

"How is the bride?" Mark asked, and I gave him a hug.

"I am wondering where my groom is." I spoke softly so no one else heard.

"He is picking up Michelle and your dad for the photos," Mark replied. I breathed a sigh of relief. My writer's brain had me thinking all kinds of awful scenarios that I would rather not consider. I lost one fiancé. I didn't want to lose this one, too.

Brooklyn and Mark had their photos taken as I waited on the side and watched how happy they were together. I heard the clacking of hooves and turned to see my dad waving from a horse drawn carriage.

It came to a stop and my dad climbed out. Then he helped Michelle out as I ran to hug them both. I went to say something, but my attention was drawn to the inside of the carriage, where my future husband was holding a sleeping baby on his chest. I knew how Chelle felt. I could sleep on his chest all day and night, too. It was hard, yet soft and safe.

The photographer's assistant carried Chelle, clad in her lilac flower girl dress, and let her sleep on her shoulder. Then Jax climbed out and within seconds I was being spun in the air. I tilted my head back and laughed, feeling free and happy.

"You make a beautiful bride, Mrs. Monroe," Jax whispered as he came in for a kiss. His velvet lips crushed mine and poured out the love he was feeling.

I started to open my lips for him when my dad yelled out, "Save it for the honeymoon!"

Jax and I both pulled away and rested our foreheads on each other's and laughed about my dad's comment. He really had a way of dousing people in ice water with his words.

"I love you, Jax," I whispered, and kissed his lips lightly.

"Let's go get married before you change your mind," he whispered with a hint of laughter.

We took all the wedding party pictures during the next half hour, with our lighthouse in the background, before the rain opened up and we all got a few drops of water on us. Then we went to the church on the opposite end of the river where the toasting farewell had taken place.

The police chaplain had immediately separated us into rooms on either side of the church. I kept peeking out the door as the church filled up with our family and friends.

"You ready?" Brooklyn asked, as she pinned a blue flower in my bouquet—a tiny forget-me-not.

"Where did this come from?" I asked quietly.

"You needed something blue, and I wanted to find a way to remember those who lost their lives. That is what this flower represents. It is for Chase, and for all the other people who have crossed our paths before their lives ended early."

I mouthed the words *thank you,* but didn't utter a sound as tears filled my eyes.

"Candice, don't cry, you will mess up your face," Brooklyn declared, and I laughed out loud at her reaction.

"Let's go get me married," I said sweetly, and Brooklyn walked with me out to the foyer.

As we came to the doors that opened to the middle aisle of the church, Brooklyn fixed my gown and my dad stared at me.

"You look like your mother," he murmured, as he tried to keep from shedding tears.

"Thank you, Daddy," I whispered, as I wrapped my arms around him and pulled him in for a hug. I was so grateful that we had healed our relationship to a point where I felt like we actually knew each other.

"You are absolutely stunning," he said, then handed me a pair of diamond earrings. "These were your mother's. I wanted you to have something borrowed and old."

I put them in my ears, then used the nearest window to see my reflection. I felt as though my mother was there with us.

Michelle walked around the corner and saw me. She immediately wrapped her arms around me and pulled me in for a hug.

"I can't thank you enough for being a mother to me all these years," I whispered into her ear.

"You were my only daughter and I love you as if you were my own. I have something for you." She reached into her purse and pulled out an ankle bracelet. "Your dad and I had this made for you. Something new."

I was in awe as I watched Michelle put it on my ankle. It had a single water drop diamond hanging off of a thin silver chain. They knew about my water wishes and how much this would mean to me. I was rendered speechless. I grabbed them both and hugged them tightly to me.

The music sounded and it was time to go. Michelle pushed Chelle down the aisle in her stroller since she was sound asleep. Then Brooklyn marched down to Canon in D minor to stand on the side and wait for me.

I linked my arm in my dad's and went to the door. I waited behind the closed doors as the music ended.

"Daddy, don't let go until you have to," I whispered, and my dad nodded his head.

The doors opened and I stepped into the spotlight that was waiting for us. I took a deep breath as the amount of people inside the church made me nervous. With everyone looking at me, I started to freak out. I closed my eyes and tried to focus as my stomach did flips.

I opened my eyes to see Jax staring at me like I was an angel. He looked at me like he was the lucky one, but I knew the opposite was true. I had done so many things wrong and could have lost him forever, but he forgave me and loved me all the same.

I focused on his smile, which seemed to light up his face and radiate joy. He looked so happy and delighted. I couldn't have been luckier than I was at that moment to have someone who looked at me like that.

As we came to a stop, the chaplain prayed. I peeked out of one open eye to see that Jax was peeking, too.

"Who presents this woman to be married to this man?" the chaplain asked.

"On behalf of all who have gathered here, and all of those not able to be with us today, I do." My dad spoke with a gravelly voice from his unshed tears. Then he gave me a kiss and put my hand in Jax's. "Take care of her, Jax."

"I won't ever let her go," he replied, then winked at me.

The chaplain said another prayer in which Jax and I never looked away from each other. Then the wedding moved forward. My mind faded down memory lane as the chaplain talked about rings and marriage. Brooklyn tapped me and took my bouquet when she handed me Jax's ring.

"Jax, I promise to love you all day, every day, for the rest of our days. I promise to make you angry and be a sore loser. I even promise to mess up the house, but I promise I will be worth the headache. I promise that there will be more good times than bad, and I will always make sure when something is bad that I give you something good to go with it. I promise to always make water wishes with you. You make me whole again, and I promise to stand by you every day for as long as we both shall live."

Then I slid the ring onto his finger. The laughter that had filled the air from my vows was almost a sigh of relief as I turned into a basket case.

"Candice, I promise to love you more than I have ever loved anyone. I promise to put you above all others. I promise to let you have the last bite of my banana split waffles. I promise that I will get you coffee every morning, and tuck you in beside me every night. I promise not to get mad when you make a mess, and I promise to make you as angry as you make me, because I can promise that I will always apologize, and I promise we will make up. I can't promise you the world, but I can promise you that I will spend my life trying to make you happy. I promise never to purposely make you cry. I love you and will love you as long as we both shall live."

Jax slid my ring on as the tears started to fall. The chaplain went on talking about how two people were becoming one, as I stared into Jax's gray eyes tinged with light blue strands. He was my wish, my water wish. He was everything I wasn't and that made us whole.

"You may now kiss the bride," the chaplain said loudly, and Jax pulled me in for a kiss. When his lips first pressed down on mine there was an odd clapping sound that made me pull away.

"Did I miss the party?"

Shivers traveled down my spine as I stared into Jax's eyes. He turned his head and then looked back at me in disbelief. I swallowed hard and closed my eyes. I knew that voice, but it wasn't possible.

Chase stood at the back of the church, while people murmured and gasped. He looked like he hadn't changed a bit. Shock reverberated through me and I wondered if this was a dream. I pulled my hand out of Jax's and pinched my arm, but I didn't wake up.

"Come on, Jax, the *bet* is over," Chase bellowed over the gasping crowd.

"Bet? What bet?"

Note from the Author

I hope you have enjoyed Book one in the Water Series, and that you do not want to throw things at me for the ending.

Book Two is out and available now.

Don't forget to follow me online for upcoming release dates. As my current project is the Brooklyn Series. Grab your copy if you haven't read it today.

AuthorElizabethYork.com
FB Page: http://goo.gl/JUeolZ
Street Team: https://goo.gl/5g9gcG
Fan Group: https://goo.gl/CMB9cb
Twitter: @AuthorEYork
Amazon Page: http://goo.gl/4grbpK

www.ingramcontent.com/pod-product-compliance
Lightning Source LLC
Chambersburg PA
CBHW070842250626
47159CB00003B/886